When Michael Skinner, head of the Skinner clan, leaps to his feet, waving the newspaper and shouting, "I've found it! I've found it!" the family is pleased but not overwhelmed. They assume he has found a job—a nice, normal one.

But of course, the Skinners never do anything that's normal. What Dad has found is not a job, but a slightly used motor home, the family's ticket to an out-of-the-ordinary trip across the country.

Calamities abound for the disaster-prone Skinners. The Great Camping Community proves a dud, and small-town America nearly does the family in. But the indefatigable Skinners weather the storms of life—and their own eccentricities—in fine style in this uproarious domestic comedy.

"A valuable 'how-not-to' guide for any family contemplating a summer spent in a 35-foot motor home, especially if the family includes four children, a large dog, and two cats....A light, funny adventure."—*School Library Journal*

By the Same Author

The Great Skinner Enterprise

........The Great........
Skinner
.........Getaway.........

Stephanie S. Tolan

PUFFIN BOOKS

PUFFIN BOOKS
Published by the Penguin Group
Viking Penguin Inc., 40 West 23rd Street, New York, New York 10010, U.S.A.
Penguin Books Ltd, 27 Wrights Lane, London W8 5TZ, England
Penguin Books Australia Ltd, Ringwood, Victoria, Australia
Penguin Books Canada Ltd, 2801 John Street, Markham, Ontario, Canada L3R 1B4
Penguin Books (N.Z.) Ltd, 182–190 Wairau Road, Auckland 10, New Zealand

Penguin Books Ltd, Registered Offices: Harmondsworth, Middlesex, England

First published in the United States of America
by Four Winds Press, Macmillan Publishing Company, 1987
Published in Puffin Books 1988
1   3   5   7   9   10   8   6   4   2
Copyright © Stephanie S. Tolan, 1987
All rights reserved
Library of Congress catalog card number: 88–42877
ISBN 0–14–032653–7

Printed in the United States of America
by Arcata Graphics, Kingsport, Tennessee
Set in Primer

For Ingrid

a friend through various strikes, enterprises, getaways
and whatever else may be waiting in the wings.

..........Contents ....

...The Great Skinner Getaway...

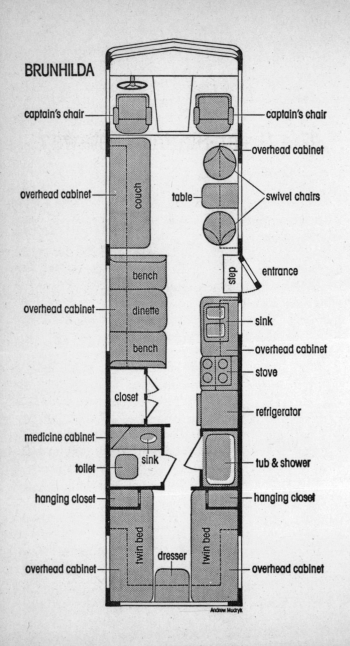

BRUNHILDA

captain's chair

captain's chair

overhead cabinet

overhead cabinet

couch

table

swivel chairs

bench

dinette

bench

step

entrance

sink

overhead cabinet

stove

closet

refrigerator

medicine cabinet

sink

toilet

tub & shower

hanging closet

hanging closet

overhead cabinet

twin bed

dresser

twin bed

overhead cabinet

Andrew Mudryk

........Introduction........
(Skip This at Your Own Risk)

Twice before I've written a book, so maybe by now it'll seem ordinary. If so, it would be the only thing about my family that is. Ordinary, I mean. That's why I'm doing this again. The other books were *The Great Skinner Strike* and *The Great Skinner Enterprise*. You have no doubt noticed the pattern in those titles, which is why I decided to call this one what I'm calling it. I like patterns. I find them comforting in the face of near chaos, which is what life in the Skinner family has been since Mom's strike.

My name is Jennifer Skinner, and I'm fifteen. In case you haven't read the other books yet, I'll list for you the rest of the family who are, of course, the main characters in our continuing story. That way you can go on with this book and get to the other two later. I'm the oldest child, followed by Ben, who has turned fourteen (and acts it). Next comes Marcia, who is eleven and almost indecently organized. The baby in the family is Rick, who's nine and a bit of a flake, but not quite such a baby anymore. As you can see, there are two adolescents in this family. Ben and I are *supposed* to be in that stage where we question who we are, rebel against authority, sometimes do crazy things, and generally cause a lot of trouble at home. But in the

Skinner family the two adults (Eleanor Jean Woodford Skinner, our mom, and Michael Richard Skinner, our dad) would give any teenager in America a run for his or her money in the identity, rebellion, and sheer craziness business. To say nothing of trouble for the family.

From their recent behavior, two rules could be learned. Mothers should not go on strike (not *ever*), even if their husbands and children don't do their fair share of the housework. There must be a better way. And fathers should not walk away from stable and secure jobs to invent a family business (at least not without prior permission from the rest of the family, i.e., the kids, who will end up having to do most of the work).

By the time this part of the Skinner story began, we'd all pretty much forgiven Mom for the agony and embarrassment of her strike. This was partly because the family contract we'd worked out at the end of it turned out to be something we could survive, and partly because it had happened so long ago that we'd practically lived it down. Dad had committed his crime much more recently. The only reason we'd been able to forgive him is that in spite of the awfulness of At Your Service while it was going on, everything turned out all right finally. Because of that business Rick has three beloved pets—two rats and a Siamese cat—and Ben has a computer. Marcia got another A+ in social studies when she wrote a report about it, and I ended up going with Jason Felton, who's a big improvement over John Bertoni. I suppose this ought to prove to us that every cloud has a silver lining. But that doesn't mean we're crazy about thunderheads.

On the sunny spring day when Dad started this part of

the story, we were ready for a rest. A lull. A calm between storms. Maybe an end to storms altogether. And this time, his idea seemed to offer just exactly that.

.......The First Step.......

Ever since he'd sold the business, Dad had been sort of at loose ends. Occasionally, he'd travel someplace to be a "consultant," but since he didn't have a regular job, he was home most of the time. I don't know exactly what he did all day, because I was in school, but partly he did his regular household jobs and most of Mom's, too. We kids noticed that he didn't do very many of *our* jobs, even though he was home with all those free hours while we were slaving away at school. We might have resented that, except that during at least part of the time he was learning how to cook. When it was his turn to make dinner, we didn't have to be afraid anymore that he'd come up with frozen turkey loaf or macaroni and cheese for the two hundredth time. But even learning to cook didn't seem to take up all his time. Sometimes, when we came home from school, he'd be in the dining room reading a book or going through the want ads in the paper.

I was always glad to see him with the want ads, because I figured it meant he was looking for a job. Ever since he and McDougal and Son (the company he used to work for) had come to a parting of the ways, I'd hoped he would find some nice, regular job like that again and go back to being a nice, regular executive who left every morning in a three-piece suit and came home in time for dinner—something calm and routine. After all, Dad's fling had been flung, he'd learned that running a family business wasn't what he wanted, and the business had been sold for a terrific profit. I thought he'd be ready to return to normal, ordinary middle-class life. I was pretty sure that's what Mom wanted, too, though I wouldn't have been willing to bet. Mom wasn't entirely predictable anymore, either.

Anyway, when Dad leaped out of his chair that sunny Sunday morning, waving the newspaper in the air and shouting "I've found it! I've found it!" I was sure "it" was a job.

Mom looked up from the *New York Times* crossword puzzle (which she always starts with great enthusiasm and never finishes) and smiled a faintly curious smile. I'd been reading a fashion article about "new-for-spring jewel-tone soft-leather skirts and jackets that no fashion-conscious woman can afford to be without," and I smiled at him, too. Rick, who was sprawled on the floor in front of the television, alternately looking at the comics and watching a Tarzan movie, didn't even seem to notice. Ben was up in his room, as usual, tapping away at his computer, and Marcia was practicing the violin for Madame Ardelle's big spring recital, so they weren't even there at the beginning this time.

"You've found a job?" Mom asked, erasing something she'd just written. (She usually gives up on the puzzle when she's erased several holes in the paper.)

"No, no," Dad said, still waving the paper as if he were fending off bats circling his head. "I've found what we're going to do for summer vacation."

Mom didn't answer for a moment as she wrote in another word. Then she looked up. "Isn't that redundant this year? You're already on vacation, it seems to me."

Dad looked offended. "I'm not the only member of this family, Eleanor. The kids are in school. You're working full-time. I think we could all use some time off."

"I'll buy that. So what is it you've found?"

"The ideal holiday concept."

Immediately, I envisioned a tropical island—and me walking in the moonlight along pure white beaches where glittering waves came and went with a soft, sighing sound. Scuba diving over coral reefs covered with brilliant anemones and entirely free of sharks; sailing one of those boats with striped sails; eating food wrapped in leaves and cooked in the ground; drinking from coconut shells—in these visions I was not alone, of course. I was with Jason Felton. Not Mom and Dad and Ben and Marcia and Rick. Only Jason Felton. Mom's voice interrupted my fantasy.

"So, what did you find? A house on the beach? A cabin in the mountains?" Mom hadn't even bothered to put down her pencil. She was still scanning the page in front of her.

"This has been a rough year," Dad said. "We need something really different."

My visions changed immediately to a camel safari across the desert, where we'd all have to eat things like boiled sheep brains and fried scorpions. That's the kind of "really different" vacation my father just might consider. With boiled sheep brains in my mind's eye, when he finally told us what he'd found, I was very relieved. Even excited. It wasn't moonlit white sand beaches, but it sounded reasonable.

"It's a motor home," he said. "A thirty-five-foot motor home in A-one condition, used only one season, and then only for two weeks and one weekend. We can have the beach and the mountains. And anything in-between."

"For rent?" Mom asked.

"For sale," Dad said.

Mom finally put down the crossword puzzle. "But, Michael, we can't afford to buy a motor home for a two-week vacation. It would cost a fortune. Several fortunes."

"But there would be no hotel bills, no restaurant bills. We'd have our accommodations with us, kitchen and all. And we could go anywhere we wanted, anywhere our fancies took us. Think of the freedom!"

"Think of the price!"

"It's used. I tell you, it's a terrific deal. And afterward, we can always sell it and get back almost all the original investment. Think of it as an investment, Eleanor."

"Think of it as a dream, Michael." Mom picked up the crossword puzzle again.

I went back to my article, only to discover that these soft-leather clothes I "had" to have cost $200 to $800 per piece. I was no more likely to have a jewel-tone leather skirt than we were to have a motor home. I dismissed both possibilities and went on to an article about the future of rock video. Dad's next words barely registered in my mind at the time.

"Well, I'll just call and make an appointment to see it anyway. It can't hurt."

A few days later I got home from school to find this enormous tan motor home in our driveway. Actually, to say "in" our driveway isn't quite accurate. It took up the whole drive, from the street clear up almost to the house. I was reminded of those science-fiction movies where people stumble on a spaceship in a field or a swamp or something, and just stand there looking at it with their mouths open.

Sarah, my best friend, was with me. She's decided to be a psychologist, and she'd brought over some books full of personality tests she wanted to use on the various members of our family. Sarah thinks Dad's going through a major midlife crisis, and she wanted to see if he showed up as crazy when identifying ink blots. Since her parents are divorced, she sort of borrows Dad for the purpose of learning about fathers.

When we saw the motor home, we stopped and stood there like zombies with our jaws hanging. Then its door opened. It was like those science-fiction movies again—you know, when somebody shouts "Look! It's opening. *Something's* coming out!" Then, slowly, the alien creature appears. What came out of the motor home, though, was just Rick, followed by Buffy, our part golden retriever.

"Jenny, wait'll you see! It's super!" Rick was grinning like a madman.

Dad appeared in the doorway, looking as proud as if he'd built the thing himself. "Come in and see it. Both of you. Marcia's inside."

As we started in, I couldn't see anything at first except Sarah's back and the stairs, which were covered with orange and brown shag carpeting. I could also see a wooden handrail. Then, after Dad had moved out of the way and Sarah was able to go on up, I got my first real look. It was astonishing. On my left there was a kitchen—wooden cabinets, a two-bowl stainless-steel sink with a window above, a four-burner stove with an oven underneath and a microwave above it, and a refrigerator. Across a carpeted aisle there was an upholstered dining area—two benches covered in a tan, velvety fabric and a table with a Formica top, by a wide window with curtains and thin blinds. Beyond the kitchen, toward the back, I could see only a wooden door. Closed.

"Well, girls," Dad said, "what do you think?"

Behind me, Rick was shoving at my rear, trying to get past.

"Oh, Mr. Skinner, it's beautiful." Sarah said. "Is it yours?"

"Not yet." I could tell from the way he said it that he fully intended it to be.

When Sarah moved, I got a chance to see the front part—the living room. On the right side were two tan-velvet upholstered chairs on swivel bases with a table between them. On the left was a couch upholstered in the same fabric, with lots of orange and brown throw pillows. There were picture windows on both sides, with more of those thin slatted blinds, and light wooden cabinets with brass handles above, next to the ceiling. Beside the upper cabinet on the right was a television, attached to the ceiling on a swivel. Ahead of all that were two captain's seats—also upholstered in the same fabric—facing the windshield. Between them was a huge carpeted bulge that must have been the engine cover. It had a wooden tray set into the top with insets for glasses. On the left was the steering wheel and a sort of cockpit that looked as if it might belong to a jet instead of a truck.

Sarah dropped her books onto the couch and sat down next to them. "It's comfortable, too," she said. "Oh, wow, this is—fantastic. It's like a regular house."

"A house you drive," Rick said. He pushed past me and threw himself onto the couch, too. "With beds and a stove and everything. And a bathroom."

Dad, resting one hand on the back of the driver's seat, was beaming. "What do you think, Jenny?"

I looked at the beautiful upholstery, the matching carpet, the curtains. "It's great," I said. "Just great."

Just then the door beyond the kitchen opened, and Marcia came out. She was beaming, too. "It works. The toilet works."

"Of course it does! Do you think they'd build these things without functional bathrooms?" Dad stepped over Sarah's feet and squeezed past me, then past Marcia. "Come on, Jenny and Sarah, and I'll show you the rest."

Marcia slid onto the bench behind the dinette table so we could get past, and we followed Dad.

The bathroom was really two little closet-sized spaces, one on each side of a narrow aisle. In one was a small toilet—"chemical," Dad explained—and a little bitty sink with a mirror and a soap dish and a toothbrush holder over it. In the other was something that looked like a cross between a big booster seat and a footbath. "Molded fiberglass," Dad said. "Seat, tub, and shower in one." The shower, I saw, was one of those portable kinds with the silver hose going up to a plastic nozzle that fits into a bracket on the wall. I couldn't imagine Dad fitting his six-foot self into that to take a shower, but he didn't seem to have any doubts.

"The way this is laid out, one person can be using the toilet while someone else is showering. These doors can either separate the two areas, or they can swing the other way to make this one big bathroom closed off from the kitchen area on one end and from the back bedroom on the other."

Sarah, trying to look over my shoulder, couldn't see very well, so I moved closer to Dad. He went on into the back bedroom and sat on one of the beds to get out of the way.

"If this were ours," he said, "you and Marcia would share this bedroom."

I went in and sat down on the other bed to make room for Sarah, who came in and stood in the aisle between the twin beds. They took up most of the space in the small room, but they looked to me like regular-sized twin beds. They had matching tan and orange and brown quilted comforters, and there was a small dresser between them on the back wall. There were windows (with both blinds and curtains) on all three sides, overhead storage cabinets, and a narrow closet. Two small lamps were fastened in the corners above the beds.

Rick came in, too. With four people in it, the bedroom was definitely full. "Show 'em where I'd sleep, Dad. Show 'em!"

So Dad maneuvered himself past Rick and Sarah, and we all went back to the living area. He reached up to the lowered ceiling above the captain's seats, punched a button, and pulled down a bunk bed, plenty big enough for Rick, providing he didn't forget where he was and try to sit up in the dark.

"The couch pulls out to a double bed," Marcia said. "Mom and Dad get that. And Ben sleeps here."

"Where? The dinette?"

"The table lowers and hooks onto the benches, and the whole thing turns into a bed."

"The manufacturer calls that a double bed," Dad said, "but I can't imagine two people bigger than leprechauns being comfortable in it. The whole thing is supposed to sleep seven. I wouldn't want to try more than six."

"That's handy," Marcia observed, "since there are six of us."

"We couldn't have guests, though," I said.

"You wouldn't take guests with you on vacation, anyway," Sarah pointed out.

"Well, gang," Dad said. "I think it's perfect, don't you?"

I looked around. It did seem to have everything. And it was sure a lot bigger than the tent we'd camped in the summer before Mom used it for her strike. Not only that, it was beautiful. And it could go anywhere.

"Perfect," I agreed.

Everyone else nodded. I glanced at Sarah, whose eyes were practically brimming over with envy, and said it again. "Just perfect."

.... Brunhilda ....

My mom spent two weeks by herself in a wilderness area when she was eighteen. She's big on roughing it—backpack and hiking boots, matches and a sleeping bag, and no more shelter than one of those teeny tents. That's how she camped out as a kid, and that's the kind of camping she prefers. Only because of us kids had she ever gone along with a camping stove, lantern, icebox, and the family-sized tent. So, much as I liked the motor home, I knew Mom would hate it.

When I heard her car drive up, I braced myself. Marcia lifted the slats of the blind behind her and looked out. "She's getting out," she reported. "She's looking it over."

Dad was trying to look unconcerned. Or confident. Whichever, it made his usual enthusiastic grin look a little lopsided.

The door opened, and Mom came up the stairs. We all held our breaths, as she looked around. For a moment, she didn't say anything. She looked first toward the living room, where we were all sitting—except Rick, who was lying on "his" bunk—and then toward the kitchen and back room. I could almost hear Dad's heart beating. She took in the sink and stove and microwave, the refrigerator, the wooden cabinets. Then she looked at Dad.

"Wow." She didn't say this. She breathed it, just like in those romance novels. Then she breathed it again. "Wow!"

"You want the grand tour?" Dad asked. His regular, normal grin had returned.

"Sure. Lead on."

The rest of us stayed where we were; there wasn't room for everybody on the grand tour. Mom's took longer than ours, because she opened drawers and cabinet doors, closed herself first into one side of the bathroom, then into the other, tried each of the twin beds. All the while, she was asking questions and Dad was answering. He explained that the refrigerator could run on gas or electricity, and that the lamps could be powered by the engine battery or by the generator when the whole system wasn't plugged in to an outside line. His voice got more and more enthusiastic.

"Do you think she'll let him buy it?" Marcia asked.

I shook my head. "No way. She'll *ooh* and *aah* and make a fuss over it, and then she'll say how much she wishes we could afford it, and then she'll say no."

So much for my gift of prophecy. When they got back to the living room, Mom's eyes were sparkling. "It's incredible!" she said. "It has absolutely everything."

"Better than a Hilton on wheels," Dad agreed.

"You really think we can afford it?"

"It's an investment," Dad said. "An investment in ourselves."

"But for only two weeks . . ."

"Two weeks is a beginning." Dad leaned against the sink, his hands in his pockets. "There are weekends, too. We'll use it a lot."

"Expensive weekends," Mom said. But I could tell by the way she was rubbing her hand over the velvet of the swivel chair next to her that she'd been won over. It had to be one of Dad's fastest victories. He'd gotten over the biggest hurdle with no problem at all. Maybe that's why Ben was such a shock.

By the time he got home from his computer club meeting, the sun was getting low in the sky and we'd turned on the lamps. Everything looked cozy and comfortable, and we were all sitting around trying to think of a name. "We can't just call it 'the motor home,' " Dad had said. "Like a boat, it needs a name."

Rick had just had his second suggestion (Rover) turned down (the first had been Richard), when Ben came up the steps. He was already frowning. His expression hadn't changed when he and Dad got back from the tour.

"What's the matter," Dad asked. "Don't you like it?"

"We buying it?"

"Yes, yes, yes," Rick said, "and we're going to name it, like a boat."

"Umph," was Ben's reaction. "I've got some stuff to do."

With that, Ben turned around and left. We all just looked at each other. How could Ben not like it?

"What's his problem?" Marcia asked.

Mom shook her head. "He's fourteen."

"Is that supposed to be an explanation?" Dad asked.

"He probably feels we made the decision without him. He probably thinks he should have had a say."

Marcia frowned. "What's the difference? Even if he'd said no, the rest of us said yes. He'd have been outvoted anyway."

Mom shrugged. "Adolescence isn't the most logical time in life."

"He'll get over it," Dad said. "Once we start talking about

where we're going and what we're going to do, he'll be as excited as anybody. Everybody out, now. I've got to take it back and tell the folks we want it."

"But the name!" Rick wailed. "We don't have a name yet."

"We'll name her at dinner."

"Her? Why her? I want it to be a boy's name!"

"Like a boat," Dad said. "Definitely female."

Sarah and I sat on the front steps for a while before she went home. "Think of sleepovers," she said.

Suddenly a whole new realm of possibilities opened up. "Privacy," I said.

"Our own little house with television, beds, bathroom . . . "

"And a refrigerator full of microwave pizzas."

"Think of parties!"

"Fantastic!"

By the time I went in for dinner, I was beginning to wonder how we'd managed to live so long *without* a motor home.

At dinner we discovered that a lot of the books Dad had been reading during his hours of free time had been about recreational vehicles. He'd also visited every RV dealer in our half of Pennsylvania, so he knew just about all there was to know. He shared all of it (considerably more than any of us cared to hear) over the meat loaf. What we were about to buy was called a "Class A Motor Home," as opposed to "trailers," "chopped downs," "put-ins," and "fifth wheels." He'd been looking for a used one for weeks and weeks when he'd found the ad.

All during Dad's lecture, none of us had much chance

to say anything, but Ben wasn't just quiet. He scowled. It was like having one nasty gray rain cloud on an otherwise glorious spring day. He even managed to keep scowling all the way through dessert, which was rocky road ice cream, his favorite. I couldn't imagine what his problem was. All last year I was fourteen, and never once had I behaved like that.

It was during dessert that we got back to choosing a name. Ben, of course, offered no suggestions. Marcia wanted Big Bertha. My suggestion was Phoenix, since the motor home was rising from the ashes of At Your Service. Rick continued to suggest only male names—King of the Road, The Beast, Bronto (for the dinosaur), and Rex. Finally, it was Mom's suggestion that won. *Brunhilda*. Rick agreed to that one when he learned it meant "armored warrior maiden."

As soon as he finished his ice cream, Ben left the table and we could hear every step as he stomped up to his room and slammed his door. Then came the sudden onset of music from the hard rock station Mom and Dad hate most.

"Whatever it is, he'll get over it," Dad said.

We didn't see *Brunhilda* for a couple of weeks after that. The previous owners had agreed to have some mechanical work done on her. Dad continued to spend a lot of time reading, though. Now it was travel books. Brochures began arriving in the mail from campgrounds and state departments of recreation. Pamphlets, maps, and guides piled up on the dining room table until it virtually disappeared. Then one Friday Mom came home like some kind of demented ballet dancer. She was bouncing and leaping and doing pirouettes clear from the front door to the kitchen, where

Marcia and I were fixing dinner and Rick was setting the table. Dad, who'd been in the dining room, followed her.

"So what happened?" he asked. "You win the lottery?"

"Two things!" Mom said, doing another pirouette between the sink and table.

"What? What? Tell us!" Marcia hates suspense.

"Bill's decided to go to Africa for the whole summer! He's given me a bonus and three months off." (Bill's the famous writer Mom works for.) "Three whole months, Michael!" I half-expected Dad to do a pirouette, too.

"You said *two* things," Marcia reminded her.

"Yes, yes. The only bad thing about three months off would be that I wouldn't be earning any money those three months. So I went to the editor of the *Gazette,* and he's hired me to write a travel column for the Sunday paper. So we can go away for the whole summer!"

"Fantastic!" Dad hugged Mom, picking her right up off the floor. "Just think of it. Three months on the road."

I thought of it. Suddenly the whole plan took on a different meaning. This would be no mere vacation. It would be three whole months. Three months sharing a tiny room with Marcia, three months away from Sarah. Worse, three months away from Jason. With no phone!

"No violin lessons!" Marcia moaned.

"No camp!" Rick wailed.

In an instant, the rest of us were on Ben's side.

Dad looked bewildered. "But it'll be the greatest adventure we've ever had!"

"What about Buffy?" Rick asked. "And Czar Nicholas and Chatter and Justin and Nicodemus. What about them?"

"Buffy can go with us," Dad said.

"What about the others?"

"We'll see."

Rick burst into tears and rushed out of the room. He has a pretty good idea of what "we'll see" means.

Mom shrugged at Dad, and he frowned at Marcia and me. "Listen here, there are kids all over the country who'd give their eyeteeth for an experience like this."

"So take *them*," Marcia muttered. I could hardly believe my ears. Marcia doesn't talk back—ever.

"What?" Mom asked.

"Never mind." Marcia, too, left the kitchen.

That left me alone with Mom and Dad and the half-set table and the half-cooked dinner. "Don't look at me," I said. "I'm not saying a word."

Dinner that night was very, very quiet.

············ Plans ············

Maybe something bigger than us wanted the trip to happen. Marcia's objection was shot down first. Madame Ardelle decided that she and her students needed a break, so she wouldn't teach violin during the summer. Once the recital was over, there would be no lessons until fall.

Mom and Dad reached a compromise with Rick about the animals. Buffy and both cats could go along, but Justin and Nicodemus, the rats, had to stay. Rick's friend Pete was recruited as rat sitter. And when Rick realized that there were zoos all over the country that we could get to in *Brunhilda,* his eagerness to go to camp disappeared.

For me, the change came a week or so later. Jason announced he'd been accepted to a six-week economics course for superbright kids at a college hundreds of miles away. He hadn't told me when he applied, in case he didn't get in; but since he had gotten in, of course, he was going. I pretended I didn't mind. Sarah pointed out that instead of sitting at home grieving over Jason's absence, I would be out on my own in a world full of other guys. "And those guys will be on vacation, too, you know, without their girlfriends. Probably feeling lonely. Everything's different in the summer, Jenny—more relaxed. More fun!"

Easy for her to say. David Wilson wasn't going anywhere all summer. And I wasn't sure I liked the idea of Jason on a college campus somewhere, feeling lonely. Still, my feelings about being away had definitely changed.

But not Ben's. Nobody knew what was the matter with Ben—he closed himself in his room with his computer and refused to discuss the summer at all.

Mom, who didn't think it was just something minor Ben would get over, kept trying to get him to talk to her. But fourteen-year-old boys can be very resistant, especially to prodding from parents. One night I heard her talking to Dad about whether they should try to find Ben a therapist. I figured even a big sister would be better than a shrink, so I took a chance and went up to his room.

He was hunched over his keyboard, playing one of those fantasy games where you talk to the computer. "Go away, Jenny," he said, without looking up. "I have to get past this killer troll."

"I'll wait." It was nearly five minutes before he turned around, but I guess he realized I wasn't going to give up.

"Okay, what's the matter?" he said finally.

"That's what I came to ask you."

He sighed. He looked at his computer, then back at me, then leaned back in his chair and looked at the ceiling. "I just don't want to go."

"Why not?"

He sighed again. "I couldn't take this." He waved at his computer.

"Sure you could. *Brunhilda* has a microwave—surely she could run a computer."

"It isn't that, Jenny. This is a delicate piece of equipment. You can't just jolt it around the country. It isn't a portable. Anyway, where would I keep it? They want me to sleep in a dinette!"

After that, he went back to his game and wouldn't say another word. I waited awhile, watching as he outwitted a goblin and found a jeweled goblet. But it was clear I wasn't going to get anything more from him. If Mom and Dad did get him a shrink, I wished the shrink luck.

There are some things you should know about Ben. He's always been sort of a loner. Before Mom's strike he was into sports, so there were lots of other kids in his life, but he wasn't really close friends with any of them. Not like Sarah and me. When he wasn't either practicing or playing a game, he spent most of his time in his workshop in the garage, inventing and building things. Then, during At Your Service, he had to drop out of sports, and he got hooked on the computer. When the business was sold and Ben got to keep the computer, he discovered all sorts of things to do with it besides programming work schedules. He discovered fantasy games or, as the software people call them, "interactive fiction." He joined a club of other computer nuts, and they played those games all the time. But I don't really think those guys were friends any more than his old teammates had been. No two ways about it, Ben is a loner.

I discussed this with Sarah. (I discuss almost everything with Sarah, since she wants to be a psychologist.) "It's probably the adolescent identity crisis," she said. "Like the mid-life crisis, only we had it first. Ben used to be The Athlete. Then he was The Computer Expert. Now maybe he's The Game Master. Maybe he doesn't know who he'd be without that computer."

She was probably right. Ben had the highest scores on those games of anybody in his club. And he'd told me once that he wanted to write the program for his own fantasy game—a harder and better one. But even if Sarah was right,

I didn't see what could be done about it. Dad kept on saying Ben would "come around." Mom didn't seem so sure.

Meanwhile, the rest of us had long meetings to plan our route. The job would have been complicated enough, given the size of the continental United States and the possible things to do and see, but Mom and Dad couldn't seem to agree on what the Getaway's main purpose ought to be. To get away, obviously. But where to? It soon became apparent that even though Mom appreciated having beds and a sink and a microwave and a bathroom, she hadn't changed her real feelings about camping. What she wanted to do was park *Brunhilda* at the edge of an unspoiled wilderness and then leave her immediately. In Mom's version of this trip, *Brunhilda* would serve as a sort of base camp and supply unit. Mostly we'd backpack and mountain climb and canoe. Anything to get us out among the deer and antelope playing.

"That's the whole point," she'd say, waving a pamphlet about wilderness trails under Dad's nose. "To *get away*— from cars and streets and smog and too many people. To experience the peace and solitude of the natural world."

"Of course the point is to get away," Dad would counter. "From the hustle and rush and stress of urban life. From people whose only goal in life is to trade up to the next-model BMW. We need to travel the back roads of America, to small towns and village greens, to find real people living real lives, accomplishing tasks that count for something, people with traditions and goals, people who build on the solid foundations of original American virtues."

Mom was not impressed. Neither was Rick, who had gone through all the travel books and located every zoo in America. His idea of the perfect trip was to start with the

Philadelphia Zoo, which was the closest, and visit every single one across the country, ending at San Diego's, which he said was not only the best zoo in America, but the best in the world.

Marcia's preference was for museums. She couldn't decide which kind of museum she liked best, so she wanted to start by going to Washington, where we could spend several days at the Smithsonian, "because it has so many different kinds." Then she thought we could plan the rest of the trip based on which of the Smithsonian's museums we liked best.

I wasn't as picky as everybody else. There would be people no matter where we went, and where there were people, some of them would surely be young and male. I'd rather have spent the summer with Jason, but since that wasn't possible, I was darned if I was going to mope around by myself.

Eventually, as usual, we reached a compromise. That is, Mom and Dad reached a compromise. They'd alternate. Sometimes we'd stop at state parks where we could get away into the woods and where Rick could see the wild animals who lived there in their natural habitat. Sometimes we'd stop in the small towns and villages where Dad's "real" Americans lived. Marcia wouldn't need museums because the towns themselves would offer sociological and historical learning experiences. They'd be endlessly interesting.

Mainly the watchword of this trip would be "flexibility." We wouldn't plan too far ahead, so we could go off in any direction that suited our fancy.

Mom worried from time to time about the cost, but that last problem was overcome when Dad ran an ad in a travel magazine, offering to rent our house. A man from Ohio wanted to spend the summer visiting all the historical sites (Independence Hall and the Liberty Bell and Gettysburg and Valley Forge) and reenacting all the famous battles that had been fought in the Philadelphia area. He agreed to rent the house until September so he could bring his family along. If Ben had been hoping for a miracle to change our plans, his hopes were shattered. With strangers living in our house, we'd *have* to get away.

Before we knew it, school was nearly over. The violin recital had come and gone (Marcia, as usual, was terrific and both she and Madame Ardelle cried when they said good-bye), and final exams had arrived. I had to study between shopping trips. It seemed as if nothing we already owned was right for this adventure. There were lists posted everywhere—lists of foods, lists of clothes, lists of cleaning supplies, bath and bed linens, cooking utensils, eating utensils, emergency needs. Marcia had even made a "list list" in case somebody forgot a whole category.

One afternoon Mom took us all out to buy hiking boots— at a cost roughly equivalent to the national debt. Then we had to have backpacks. Mom got these huge aluminum frame packs for herself and Dad. She'd have gotten them for the rest of us, too, but when she and the salesman put a partially packed one on Rick, he fell over on his back and lay there, kicking like a June bug. Mom decided we could all make do with day packs. "At least at first, we can come back to *Brunhilda* at night." I couldn't imagine why anyone would buy a motor home and *not* plan to come back to sleep in it every night, but I didn't say anything. Ben's attitude had gotten on Mom's and Dad's nerves to the point that none of the rest of us dared make even the teeniest suggestion or hint at a complaint. What we did was smile and nod a lot.

The Smith family (the ones who were renting our house) was due to arrive the Sunday morning after school got out, so that last week things got really hairy. Buffy, who always knew when someone was getting ready to go away even for a weekend, was beside herself with excitement. If someone got out a suitcase, she'd sit next to it, or on it, or in it. Every time anybody opened the door, she flew out and sat in front of *Brunhilda*. If *Brunhilda*'s door got opened, she went inside and refused to come out again. Chatter, the Siamese cat Rick had gotten from one of his At Your Service clients, followed us around the house, meowing steadily. Rick said she was offering advice. I think the level of activity had driven her to the edge of a nervous breakdown. I sympathized. Even Czar Nicholas, whose most strenuous exercise is usually his once-a-day walk from the living room to his supper dish in the kitchen, caught the general feeling. We kept finding him inside paper bags that had just been emptied, or climbing around on the piles of things that had turned the front hall into an obstacle course.

Friday, the last day of school, Jason walked me home and we stood outside the back door for a while to be alone.

"Can I write to you? How will I know where you'll be?" Jason asked.

"There's a mail-forwarding service. I'll give you their address."

"Good. And you'll write, too."

"Sure."

"You want to go to a movie tomorrow?"

"If Dad'll let me. Tomorrow's the final organizing and packing day."

"I'll call you later."

"Okay."

It was just then, just when Jason was about to kiss me, that Ben came crashing out the back door, practically running us down on his way to the garage, where he jerked open the door to his old workshop and disappeared inside, slamming the door behind him. I don't think he even noticed us. Dad did, though. He came out the back door about two seconds later, practically breathing fire.

"Where'd he go?"

I pointed to the garage, and Jason and I stepped out of the way as Dad stormed after Ben.

"And just exactly what do you expect to do instead, Benjamin Woodford Skinner?" Dad boomed as he reached for the door handle.

There was no sound from inside the garage. Dad jerked at the door, but it didn't open. "Ben, unlock the door this minute!"

No answer.

"*Ben!*"

"I think I'd better go," Jason whispered, and took off.

Mom appeared at the back door. "Michael, come inside."

"Open the door!" Dad repeated.

"Michael, come in and let him alone. We'll deal with this later."

Dad gave one more pull on the door and then went back in. I waited a suitable interval and then followed. Rick and Marcia were in the kitchen.

"What happened?"

"Ben's not going with us," Rick said.

"Yes he is." Mom appeared from the front hall.

"Well, that's what he said."

"I heard what he said." Mom's voice was surprisingly calm. "But he's going with us, and that's all we need to say about that."

Ben stayed in the garage right through dinner, and Mom didn't even tell him to come in. I figured she had a plan. Sure enough, while Dad and I were doing the dishes she went out and shut herself in the garage with him. After a while they came back, and even though he was still pretty grumpy, it was clear he was going to go along. As we approached final countdown, at least all six Skinners were getting away

.... Countdown ....

Saturday was packing day. Morning was for personal packing, afternoon for loading *Brunhilda*. When Jason called and suggested we go to McDonald's for lunch, I agreed. I was sure I could get my packing done in an hour or two, at most. Sarah came over early, and we stood in my room, with all my summer clothes spread out around us, trying to decide what I should take. "Pack light," Dad had said. "Two bags per person, max!" Two bags seemed plenty. Ben's suitcase and duffel bag were already outside his closed bedroom door.

"First, shorts," Sarah said. "The peach ones are my favorites."

"Mine, too." I put my peach shorts on the bed. "This will be the 'take-along' pile." I put my old white shorts on the floor. "And this will be the 'reject' pile."

Fifteen minutes later the "take-along" pile completely covered my bed. The "reject" pile contained my white shorts and a halter top that didn't match anything else. And I hadn't even gotten to the jeans and other warm clothes.

"Maybe we should start with jeans this time," Sarah suggested. She swept everything off onto the floor, and we began the take-alongs with two pairs of blue jeans.

"The white ones, too," I said. "For dressier."

29

"A long-sleeved shirt and a sweatshirt," I said, adding them to the new pile.

"Ooh, Jenny, not that old navy thing. Take your pink sweatshirt."

"For hiking? It'll get dirty."

"It looks so much better." I put both sweatshirts on the pile.

"Take your plaid shirt," Sarah said.

"The yellow one's enough."

"But it doesn't go with the pink sweatshirt. The plaid's much better."

I added the plaid shirt. "I should have something dressy."

"So take the yellow sundress."

"And sandals."

"Right. You have to have sandals."

"And running shoes and the hiking boots."

"Are you taking your tennis racket?"

"Sure."

"So tennis shoes and white shorts . . ."

"But the white shorts are practically the only thing on the reject pile."

Sarah sighed. "All right, so you could play tennis in the peach ones. Let's see now—bathing suit. That doesn't take up much room."

"They don't," I corrected. "There's the one-piece I got when Mom went shopping with me and the bikini I bought for myself when I still thought I'd be spending the summer with Jason."

"And don't forget your beach robe—and your flip-flops."

In another fifteen minutes we were right back to a bed full of clothes to take along and almost nothing to leave at home.

"Maybe we'd better start with nonwearable items," Sarah said. "Curling iron."

"Hair dryer."

"Hair brush, styling brush, comb . . ."

"Styling mousse, spray . . ."

"Zit cream, complexion soap, cotton balls, isopropyl alcohol, shampoo . . ."

"Toothpaste, toothbrush, floss . . ."

"Makeup, emory boards, nail polish . . ."

"Sarah, I can go into the wilderness without nail polish."

Sarah winced. "All right, but I don't see why a teeny little bottle like that should be a problem."

I shook my head. "One has to draw the line somewhere. Now, is that all?"

"Typewriter, pens, pencils, and paper."

"What for?"

"Jenny, don't you think a whole summer with the Skinner family in a motor home is going to *have* to be recorded for posterity?"

"Okay. And stationery and envelopes and books to read." I took my Tolkien Middle Earth poster down from the wall. "And this. If I put it up in Marcia's and my room it will make me feel at home."

"Too bad you can't take Foof." Foof is my four-foot-tall purple teddy bear.

"I know. But if I took him, Marcia would have to stay home. I'll put him in the attic," I said. "The renters wouldn't appreciate him."

We gathered everything we'd listed. I shook my head. "We are *never* going to get all this into two suitcases!"

"Maybe Marcia has some extra room in one of hers."

So we went to Marcia's room. It was almost as bad as

mine. Marcia was standing in the middle, her hands on her hips and a frown on her face.

"Are you kidding?" she said when I asked her. "I have more than two bags' worth myself."

"My clothes alone would fill a steamer trunk," I said.

"Clothes? Clothes are easy. I'm just taking two of everything. But do you think they'll let me take my violin?"

"Sure they will." I noticed the huge pile of books at the foot of her bed. "But they won't let you take your encyclopedia."

"I know. But what if I need to look something up? There aren't any libraries in the woods."

"There are in the towns and villages."

"Probably not good ones."

"Every library in America has an encyclopedia," Sarah pointed out.

"I guess so. But I won't like being without my own."

"It's called roughing it."

Marcia, too, had lots of paper and pencils and pens. Also a battery-operated pencil sharpener, graph paper, ruler, compass, eraser, scissors, notebooks, a stapler, tape, paper clips, rubber bands, and file folders, all piled into the briefcase Mom and Dad had given her for sixth-grade graduation. "I can't get the darned thing closed," she complained. "And I haven't even put any books in yet."

"It looks as if you're getting ready to go off to college," Sarah observed. "Are you taking that dictionary?"

"Of course!"

"Can't you manage with a little paperback one?" I asked.

She shook her head and I didn't argue. "How're you going to manage with just two pairs of shorts? What happens when they both get dirty?"

"Where there are libraries, there are Laundromats. Anyway, if I have to, I can always wash things by hand. *Brunhilda* does have water and a sink."

"Come on, Sarah, let's try again. Maybe taking two of everything will work."

It didn't. We started over five more times, and then Jason was there to take me to lunch, and I had to tell him I couldn't go. We'd finally cut down to bare essentials, but they filled both my allotted bags, and I still had to figure out what to do with my hair dryer and my cosmetics and all that. I sent Jason to see if he could do anything to help Dad, while Sarah and I went back to see if we could squeeze in anything more.

When hunger drove us downstairs, we had managed to pack almost everything. All that was left over was my terrycloth beach robe, my shoes, books, and the portable typewriter.

The kitchen was worse than my room. The table and countertops were covered. There were canned foods on one counter, boxed foods on another, bags of potatoes, onions, carrots, and celery on the table. There was a section for baking items, one for condiments, and another for cleaning supplies. The lists taped to the refrigerator were all checked off. The kitchen looked like a well-stocked supermarket.

"Can't we stop at a store every day or something?" I asked. "Do we have to take all this?"

Mom's nerves must have been wearing thin. "Of course we don't have to take all this," she said. "I just thought I'd get everything out so we could have the fun of putting it all away again!"

Sarah and I decided not to ask about lunch. We went outside and found that Dad and Jason had gone to

McDonald's in *Brunhilda*. They were just getting back.

"Guess what we discovered," Jason said when he climbed out, his arms full of big white paper bags. "*Brunhilda* doesn't fit in the drive-through."

Dad, with more bags, came around the front. "It's a good thing Jason was with me, or we might have come home with half their roof."

"Or without *Brunhilda*'s."

Dad laughed. "We could have peeled it back like a sardine can. I was already in line when Jason asked how tall we were. We had to back out."

"Your dad's great at backing that monster," Jason said. "I was impressed."

"Thank you. You're pretty good at directing traffic."

"That policeman helped."

"Okay, gang, let's eat and we'll start loading. You all packed, Jenny?"

Sarah and I both nodded. We were close enough. I figured we could put the rest in a paper bag and hide it among the kitchen stuff.

After lunch Jason went home, promising to come back later to take me to a movie. Sarah stayed. First Dad had everybody bring down their two allotted bags. Marcia had managed to get everything into hers, but I could tell from the way she came down the stairs—with a decided tilt—that one of them weighed a ton. Ben's stuff had been packed since the crack of dawn. Rick had the smallest bags because Mom had packed for him. One of his bags contained clothes; the other, bigger one, had toys.

When our eight bags plus Mom and Dad's two big ones were down with everything else, the whole front hall was jammed, and there was more in the dining room, to say nothing of the stuff in the kitchen. Looking like an African safari, we started taking it all out and piling it next to *Brunhilda*. The pile was impressive.

When we started taking it inside, we found out how small a Class A Motor Home really is.

When you stand in the middle of *Brunhilda,* you see all these doors that make it seem as if she's lousy with storage space. This is not an entirely accurate perception. Dad took Rick's bags in and pulled open one of the lower doors.

"Is that where I put my clothes or my G.I. Joes?" Rick asked.

Dad closed the door and stood up. "It's where they put the water tank." There were also doors in front of the compressor for the refrigerator, the gas tank and lines for the stove, the plumbing for the sink, and the wheel wells. Where it looked as if there were cabinets, there was barely room for a pair of socks. In the living room, *Brunhilda* had only the overhead bins, which weren't all that big. Luckily, beneath the closet that was across from the refrigerator there were three big drawers. Dad unpacked Rick's clothes into the bottom one and still managed to get it closed.

"Do I get one of these?" Ben asked. Sarah and I were at that moment trying to figure out how to get even my underwear into one of the narrow drawers in the teensy dresser between Marcia's and my beds.

"Your mother and I need these two," Dad said. "You can share the girls' dresser."

I shrieked, but Dad was not understanding. There were two of us and three drawers, and he didn't care what size they were. Ben was to have one of them. When Ben brought

his duffel bag to our room I figured that if he took everything
out of it, the duffel bag itself could *maybe* fold up small
enough to fit into the third drawer.

"Where do my G.I. Joes go?" Rick asked.

"Put them on the couch for now." Dad sighed so loudly
we could hear him in our room.

Mom had really packed light, so she managed to get all
her clothes into her drawer and the closet without even
reaching the sighing stage. But then she started bringing
in the kitchen stuff. After two trips she had used up the
slide-out rack called the "pantry," the drawers for silver-
ware, the half-cabinet under the sink, and the cupboard
overhead. She skipped the sighing stage altogether.

"Michael!" she yelled. "What do they expect you to do
with the food—tie a pack mule on behind?"

Dad, who'd been trying to fit the rainy-day games into a
bin over the couch, shrugged. "You aren't supposed to keep
anything in the galley except staples."

"What do you think I'm bringing, caviar and canned
crab? These are staples."

"How about the closet?"

"You want me to put the flour in your tennis shoes?"

Back in our room, Marcia, Sarah, and I knew exactly how
she felt. We couldn't really afford the space for the beds.
Even with all the overhead bins stuffed full, I hadn't been
able to unpack one of my suitcases or my grocery bag.
Marcia had filled all her bins with just half of her heavier
bag. Her violin and briefcase were in the drawer under her
bed, and with her underwear in her one dresser drawer,
she still had all the rest of her clothes to dispose of somehow.

"I know!" she shouted suddenly, and began to rip the
bedding off her bed. When she reached the bare mattress,

she began laying her shirts and shorts and jeans out carefully on it. Then her sweaters, her sweatshirt, her jacket and her socks. When the mattress was completely covered and her suitcase empty, she carefully put the bottom sheet back over everything, smoothed it out, and finished making the bed.

Sarah, who was sitting on my bed to stay out of the way, shook her head. "Ingenious!"

"But everything'll get wrinkled!" I protested.

"We're going to the woods. Wrinkles don't matter in the woods," Marcia said.

Luckily we had a miniature closet so I could hang up my sundress and blouses. Sarah switched to Marcia's bed, and I laid my jeans and sweatshirts and shorts out on my mattress. Then, since Ben had taken his duffel bag and disappeared, I put my bathing suits and suntan lotion in the third drawer. Even so, I still had tons of stuff I couldn't squeeze in anywhere.

Several times that afternoon things had to be taken out of where they'd been put when somebody discovered that something else more important had to be there. Mom decreed that in the bathroom cabinet there would be only one tube of toothpaste everybody would use (Rick had a fit that it wasn't his pump container of candy-tasting stuff none of the rest of us could stand), one bar of soap, one shampoo, etc. It was clear that in a motor home efficiency was more important than individuality.

When every nook and cranny had been crammed full— you'd be surprised what can fit in and around a plumbing system—we all stood outside, surrounded by everything else.

"I'm going to go buy a couple of those rooftop carriers,"

Dad said. "I didn't think we'd need them."

"Will that hold the rest of this?" Marcia asked.

"Most of it."

"Most?" Rick said.

"Most?" I echoed. There were things in that pile that could be considered nonessential only in a post-nuclear-war survival situation. "Isn't there room in the outside compartments?"

Dad lifted the doors. Inside were fishing poles, the lantern, everybody's hiking boots, tennis rackets, the mini-vacuum cleaner Dad had bought at an RV store, Mom's portable typewriter (I'd given mine up), the badminton and lawn dart sets, and the box of emergency road equipment. There was maybe room for a toothpick.

"What kind of a family was this made for?" Marcia asked.

"Small," Sarah said.

Smaller, it seemed, than the Skinners.

When Jason came over to take me to a movie, we never even asked if we could go. Instead, Jason spent our last romantic evening with Dad on top of *Brunhilda*, fastening down the new carriers (called "clamshells") and then climbing up and down the ladder, taking up the stuff that had to be packed in them. Ben, who should have been doing all that, was nowhere to be seen.

We did manage to get very nearly everything in, though. By the time Jason kissed me good-night and went home, we were almost ready. I hardly thought about what a weird last date it had been. I was too excited about the trip.

I was not, however, as excited as Rick, who got up twice during the night and threw up.

...... We Have Liftoff ......

We were all up and doing early the next morning. This was not only launch day, it was also "get ready for the Smiths" day. Mom wanted our house to look like a spread in one of those house-and-garden magazines. You'd have thought we were trying to sell it instead of getting it ready for renters. Marcia's job was to dust the downstairs, I was to vacuum, Ben was to put anything we didn't want the Smith family to use in the attic storage space, and Rick had to clean the bathrooms. Dad went to get doughnuts.

Mom was making little notes to put up everywhere. She had notes to explain how to use the washer and dryer and the VCR, notes telling where the fuse boxes were and how to fix the water heater if the pilot light went out, notes about weeding the flower garden and feeding the wild birds. There was also a list of phone numbers of important people like the plumber and the hospital emergency room, the police, fire department, and Mrs. Anderson, our next-door neighbor. And she'd drawn up a map to show how to get to the nearest grocery and drugstore.

Buffy took up a position by the front door, leaping up with wildly wagging tail the minute anyone came near it. When Dad arrived with the doughnuts, she tore out between his legs to stand guard by *Brunhilda*. She was not going to be left behind.

We stopped halfway through our various jobs to eat, and
as we were finishing the last of the doughnuts, with the
boxes and papers and sugar and crumbs all over the kitchen
table, Buffy started to bark. She kept it up and kept it up.

"When are they supposed to get here?" Marcia asked.

"Not till noon," Mom said. "They can't be here yet. Rick,
go see what she's barking at."

Rick went. "They're here," he said when he got back.
"At least somebody is. Buffy won't let them out of the car."

"What?" Dad went roaring out, with the rest of us (except
Mom, who was madly gathering up doughnut mess) right
behind him.

A red station wagon, nearly covered with bumper and
window stickers, piles of suitcases, and two big wheels tied
on top, was parked in front of the house, and Buffy was
standing with both paws on the rear passenger door, barking ferociously. Though the windows were rolled up, we
could hear a kind of barking echo from inside. A bulldog's
already flat face was mashed against the glass. The dogs
were sort of barking into each other's teeth.

"Buffy, get down!" Dad commanded, with all the effect
of a whistle in a windstorm. He grabbed her by the collar,
dragged her away, and shoved her into *Brunhilda*.

Immediately, the driver's door popped open and Mr.
Smith got out fast, slamming the door behind him to keep
the bulldog in.

"Sorry about that . . ." he and Dad both said at the same
time, then stopped and laughed.

"Buffy doesn't usually behave that way," Dad said.

"Oh, that's all right. Duke always does." Mr. Smith was
short and wide, and reminded me a lot of that bulldog of
his, except his face wasn't so flat. He had red hair and big

hands, and a voice that could be heard about three blocks away.

"Do you have a place I could chain Duke up while we get settled in?"

Dad had Rick show Mr. Smith where he could hook Duke's chain to the garage door. Without Buffy there, the dog seemed perfectly well behaved. In fact, I thought he was cute—a sort of ugly cute. Rick couldn't be persuaded to leave him once he was chained. He said he felt sorry for him, tied up all alone in a new place.

Then Mrs. Smith, who looked to me exactly like the Mrs. Butterworth syrup bottle, and the two Smith children got out of the car and stood in the front yard, waiting to be introduced. They had a long wait. Mr. Smith was busy greeting Mom, who had given up trying to get the whole house finished and come outside. Mr. Smith took both her hands in his and shouted at her how glad they all were to be here and what a fine house we had and what a fine motor home *Brunhilda* was and how grateful he and the little missus and the crumb-grabbers were that they could rent our house. Then he shouted about the fine motel they'd stayed in the night before and how close it was, which was why they were so early, and how they'd driven through Gettysburg yesterday and had thought it was just fine and could hardly wait to get back and map it out so they could walk all around it and "relive" the battle. Somewhere in there he took a breath and then went on about what a fine trip they'd had out from Ohio and how many fine places they'd stopped at along the way, all of which had had bumper stickers for their collection.

This greeting seemed to take about a year, after which he introduced the missus and the crumb-grabbers. He

never did call his children by their names. After the intro-
duction, Mrs. Smith started in, with a much smaller voice,
but just as steadily. She told Mom how lovely our house
was and how much like it their house at home was, and
how they'd rented that to a lovely family whose house had
burned down. "*What* a sad story that was, just a *tragedy*!"
She told how those poor folks had lost everything, so it was
just providential that they, the Smiths, were coming out
here to Philadelphia and could let them have their house
for the summer, and then she said how anxious she was
to see just everything in our lovely house.

In no time the adult Smiths, still talking, had disappeared
inside with Mom and Dad, and Marcia and I were left
staring at the crumb-grabbers, who were round, pale, red-
headed children who looked almost exactly alike except that
one wore jeans and the other a dress. I assumed they were
a boy and a girl, so close to the same size they might have
been twins, somewhere between six and eight, maybe.
They didn't seem capable of speech. Marcia said hello and
asked them their names, but they just stood and stared at
her. Maybe they didn't have names. I figured they never
had a chance to get a word in edgewise with their parents.
Besides, they were probably already worn out by their fine
and lovely vacation. I doubted it was the kids who wanted
to map out the whole battle of Gettysburg and relive it. We
had a pretty uncomfortable few minutes staring at each
other, and then Mr. Smith came out and shouted that the
kids should come in and see their rooms, so we all went
inside.

The boy was to have Ben's room, and the girl was to have
mine. Marcia's wasn't going to be used at all, which was
just as well because no child could live in Marcia's room

without messing something up (which would give Marcia a heart attack) and in mine it just wouldn't matter. Foof was already safely tucked away in the attic. Rick's attic room wasn't going to be used, either. It had taken on a distinct smell of rat that hadn't disappeared after Rick, crying all the way, had taken Justin and Nicodemus over to Pete's for the summer. Ben had put his computer up in Rick's room and then put a padlock on the door. He was afraid the Smith children would break in and wreck it, and he was threatening to sue if they did.

The Smith kids didn't say anything about their new rooms, either. They just sat down on the beds and stayed, each in his or her place, while their parents brought up their belongings. They didn't look like kids who'd break open a padlock and wreck a computer. I almost wished I'd left Foof to keep the poor, little, silent crumb-grabbers company.

Having the Smith family there so early put sort of a strain on the last moments of getting ready to leave. The vet had given us some cat tranquilizers for the trip. Mom decided to give the cats the pills right away and put them into their cat carriers so they'd be out of the way. Czar Nicholas was a snap. She put his pill in a bit of canned cat food and he gobbled it right down. Chatter, on the other hand, suspected something. She looked at the little glob of her favorite food and then at Mom and went and climbed the dining room curtains. When we got her down, Mom tried a couple more times, then had me hold her while she shoved the pill down her throat with the eraser end of a pencil. When that little operation was finished I had claw marks on both arms and Chatter was hysterical. This condition did not improve when we put her into her carrier. The whole rest of the morning was accompanied by Chatter's loud meowing as she tried to rip, chew, and claw her way out through her carrier's air holes.

Mom and Marcia went around checking things off the last-minute lists. We gave up finishing the cleaning. We'd expected to be ready to leave when the Smiths arrived, so that we could do a final sweep through the house to see what we might have left behind. But now it was hard to keep straight what was the Smiths' stuff coming and what was ours going.

Sarah and Jason came over around eleven-thirty to say good-bye. When they arrived, we were almost ready. The folding lawn chairs were tied on the roof; the piles of last-minute things had all been squeezed in somewhere. The cat carriers, Chatter's still sounding as if an ax murder were going on inside, had been stowed on Marcia's and my beds in *Brunhilda*. Mom was offering advice to the Smiths (banks to use, cheap gas stations, and so on) and essential information like the phone number of the campground we were going to that night and the address of the mail-forwarding service. Dad was up and down and around *Brunhilda*, checking to be sure that everything was stowed securely.

Jason had brought a bottle of ginger ale with aluminum foil on the top to make it look like champagne. "For the launch," he explained. Because we couldn't very well break the bottle on *Brunhilda*'s bumper, we opened it and passed it around as a kind of toast to the Getaway.

Mrs. Anderson, from next door, came over to say good-bye and meet her new temporary neighbors. She left her

four-year-old terrorist-in-training daughter, Amy, at home
(probably to avoid frightening the Smiths), but she brought
a grocery bag she'd packed with lunch. "This is so you
won't have to stop today," she said, as she handed the bag
to Mom. Mom said we didn't have to stop to eat in *Brunhilda,* but Mrs. Anderson said she thought we should get
safely set up for the night somewhere before trying out the
kitchen. Mom thanked her for her thoughtfulness. Later it
was clear that Mrs. Anderson knew something we didn't.

And then there was nothing left to do but say good-bye,
climb into *Brunhilda,* and go. I hugged Sarah, hugged and
kissed Jason, and went straight back to my bed so nobody
would see that I was crying. As Dad started *Brunhilda,* I
raised the blinds and waved. Sarah was crying, too. Jason
wasn't. Mrs. Anderson and the Smiths stood on the lawn
and waved and yelled, "Bon voyage!" Buffy was barking,
and so was the bulldog. All we needed was a band playing
and streamers flying.

Dad maneuvered *Brunhilda* out of the driveway, got her
headed in the right direction on the proper side of the street,
and we were on our way. I could almost hear a voice saying,
"We have liftoff." I watched Jason and Sarah until we
turned at the end of the block.

It was strange to sit there on my bed, in a room with my
Middle Earth poster on the wall, while the old familiar
houses of our neighborhood went by outside the window.

Chatter was still working away at the air holes in her
carrier with all her claws, and still meowing. There was no
sound from Czar Nicholas's cage—and no paws sticking
out, either. I peeked inside. He was sound asleep in spite
of Chatter's noise. It was too much for me, though, so I
went to join the rest of the family.

Ben was sitting at the dinette table, reading a paperback book. Marcia was on the couch. Dad turned a corner, and I got thrown against the sink. Clearly, walking around while *Brunhilda* was moving was going to take some getting used to.

"Where's Rick?" I asked.

Mom turned around. She looked from Marcia to Ben to me. "In the bathroom?" she asked.

I shook my head.

"Michael, stop!" she said, her voice so sudden and loud that Dad slammed on the brakes. *Brunhilda* stopped. I didn't. Not until I reached the living room, where I tripped over Buffy and fell on top of Marcia. Ben's book flew clear from the dinette table to the engine cover, and there were ominous thumps from all the storage bins.

"Don't startle me like that," Dad said. "Somebody could have gotten hurt."

"Somebody did," Marcia moaned from under my left elbow.

"Rick's not here!"

"What do you mean, he's not here?" Dad had started moving again, and Marcia and I untangled ourselves.

"He's not here. We left him!"

"How could we have left him? Where was he?"

"Last I saw him, he was messing around with that bulldog," Marcia said.

"Same here," Ben said.

"We have to go back." This was Mom.

"Of course we have to go back," Dad said. "It isn't like forgetting a toothbrush. What do you think I'm doing?"

What he was doing was turning right at the next corner. But in the stress of the moment, he apparently forgot what he was driving. He took the corner as if we were in Mom's Maverick. There was a jolt, as the right back wheel went up over the curb, then a thud, a crunch, and a scraping sound. We stopped again, a little less suddenly than before, but not much.

"What happened?" Mom asked.

Dad didn't answer. He just climbed out and went around to the back. When he got back in, he was shaking his head. "Just a scrape. It could have been worse."

"What happened?"

"We got the telephone pole." He restarted the engine. "Let's everybody try to keep calm, now."

Chatter wasn't making it any easier to keep calm. All the bumps had apparently further unnerved her. Now she was shrieking. I went and closed the door to the room, then the bathroom door, so that the sound was muffled at least a little. Clearly, Rick's cat was not going to make this trip any easier. Then I remembered. "I know where Rick went!" I said. "He went to Pete's to say good-bye to Justin and Nicodemus."

So instead of having to go back home after our dramatic launching, which would have been embarrassing, we drove to Pete's. Sure enough, Rick was there. He thought it was nice of us to come pick him up. Nobody wanted to hurt his feelings, so we didn't admit that we'd gone off and left him. When Rick was safely aboard, Pete and his mother gave us another sendoff, and we were finally, truly on our way— a little late, a little frazzled, and with a new scrape and dent in *Brunhilda*'s beautiful exterior, but on our way. The Getaway had begun.

Despite Rick's pleas that he was dying of starvation, Mom

refused to hand out any of Mrs. Anderson's sandwiches until we'd gotten out on the interstate. I think she wanted to be able to concentrate all her energies on driving. She didn't have a steering wheel, brakes, or an accelerator, but you could tell she was using every muscle in her body to keep *Brunhilda* properly on the road. Once we were out of town and on the highway, she relaxed a little. She got the bag out from under her seat and began pulling out foil packages. "Here, Rick," she said, holding two of them out. "You take them around."

While Rick was maneuvering around Buffy to give Ben and me our sandwiches, Mom unwrapped another, put a napkin around it, and handed it across to Dad. Then she gave Rick one for Marcia and one for himself. Dad, taking a bite, swerved slightly, and Rick caught himself on the chair with the hand that was holding his sandwich. Mayonnaise squirted out all over the tan velvet chair seat. At the same moment Dad announced that he had egg salad, which he hated, Ben shouted that he wasn't eating peanut butter on rye bread, and I discovered that mine was salami and cheese made with ketchup instead of mustard.

"Stop, Michael," Mom said—more gently this time.

Dad put on the blinkers and pulled off onto the shoulder of the road, while we got lunch straightened out and the chair cleaned up. Buffy got Rick's smashed tuna salad, Mom took Dad's egg salad, Ben traded with me, and Marcia kept hers, which was also peanut butter on rye. Luckily, Mrs. Anderson had put in some extras, which Rick and Dad took. They were also salami and cheese and ketchup. There were also some plums and little boxes of fruit juice. Dad wanted to get going again as soon as everybody had something to eat, but Mom said she wasn't having anyone eating or drinking, even from a closed box with a straw, while we were moving. Now that we were stopped, it was very much quieter, and the noise from the back bedroom was awful.

"I thought you gave those cats tranquilizers," Dad said.

"I did," Mom answered. "But I'd forgotten what the vet told me."

"Which was?"

"That cats are hard to prescribe tranquilizers for. It doesn't work the same way on all of them."

"You mean it takes more than one pill for some? You'd better give those creatures another. How about two or three more?"

Mom took a bite of her sandwich, chewed, and swallowed before she answered. "It's not the dose. It's just that it works the opposite way on some cats."

"Do you mean that just before we started a five-hour drive, you gave those cats *uppers*?"

Mom nodded. "I meant to experiment last week, to see how they reacted. But we were so busy, I forgot."

"Wonderful. How long do the pills last?"

"I don't know."

We found out. A long, long time.

When we got back on the road again, Dad turned on the radio, which had speakers in the front and also back in Marcia's and my bedroom. The music and the engine noise helped cut down the cat sound. I went back to our room again, and with the music, it wasn't too bad. I moved Czar Nicholas's carrier onto Marcia's bed with Chatter's and stretched out on mine. I hadn't slept much the night before, and I was wiped out. Besides, the movement of a car always makes me sleepy, so—in spite of Chatter and the radio—I zonked.

By the time I woke up and lurched my way forward, racking my hip on the dinette table as I went by, it was late afternoon. Rick was stretched out on the couch, asleep; Marcia was in one armchair, watching the scenery; and Ben was in the other armchair, still reading that book. Buffy was stretched out at their feet, taking up every speck of available floor space. I was left with the dinette. Mom was looking intently at a large, unwieldy road map.

"I told you, I thought you should take that last exit," Mom said.

"It said Connorville, not Mervin. We want to get off at Mervin." It didn't sound to me as if this was the beginning of their conversation.

"But we want Route 5. And it did say Route 5."

"East. It said Route 5 east. We want west."

"I don't think it said east or west. It just said Route 5."

"We want the next exit, Ellie. You'll see. Route 5 west."

Mom rattled the map a few times, but she didn't answer. I couldn't see out very well from where I was, but Marcia could. She was shaking her head.

"There!" Mom said, and rattled the map again. "That exit says Route 233."

Dad didn't answer. He kept driving straight ahead.

"Michael, where are you going? We're not going to get to Route 5 by going any farther."

"Route 5 isn't the only rcad in the state, Ellie. We'll get there another way."

"What way?"

"Route 12."

"But that's miles out of the way."

"It's no farther than turning around and going back to

Route 5. We'll just come up to the park from the rear. Trust me, Eleanor."

We passed two more exits before one said Route 12, and Dad took that one onto the narrowest, windingest road I'd ever seen. There were places where *Brunhilda* seemed to take up the whole road. If someone had come around a curve toward us, they'd have had to go off the pavement to keep from being squashed, except that there were no shoulders—just trees. I was surprised a road this small even had a number. I turned around so that my back was to the windshield. If we were going to crash, I didn't want to know about it beforehand.

Route 12 went on forever. Or maybe it was that we had to go about thirty miles an hour. Anyway, dusk was coming on and everybody was hungry again, and there hadn't been so much as a sign for the park. Cars kept getting caught behind us and honking at us to move so they could get by. With all the curves in the road, there were hardly any passing zones—it was all double yellow lines. Every so often Dad would find a wide place where he could pull over enough to let the cars go by, their drivers or passengers shaking their fists and making rude gestures. Rick woke up and started complaining that he was hungry again. Mom produced a bag of potato chips and it was gone in a flash. Buffy started to whine and pace up and down the narrow aisle, so Dad had to find another wide spot to pull over so we could let her out for a few minutes. By the time Buffy was back in, it was getting dark. Still no sign of the park.

Finally the headlights illuminated a huge brown sign. "There it is. I told you we could get here this way."

Mom folded her map noisily. I thought it was noble of

her not to point out that we were nearly three hours late in arriving. We stopped at the little booth where the park ranger was.

"You folks're gettin' here pretty late," the ranger said. "Do you have a reservation?"

"Of course." Dad held out our reservation slip. "We expected to get here before dark."

"First day out?"

Dad nodded.

"Yessir, it always takes longer to get started than you think it will. Only gonna stay with us the one night, I see."

"We like to stay loose."

"If you want to stay longer, let us know as soon as possible, sir. We fill up fast. Here you go, you're in 18-A." He showed Dad on a little map how to get to our site, took the money Dad handed him, and gave us a sticker to put in the window. "Okay, folks, no open fires, use the fireplaces, no cutting trees, buy firewood at the camp store, pets on a leash at all times, no loud music, no washing dishes in the bathrooms, checkout time eleven-thirty, all trash in cans." He said this list fast, the way a waitress lists twenty kinds of ice cream, then took a breath. "Enjoy your stay," he finished.

Dad drove very slowly, trying to find site 18-A. The numbers were on little posts that were hard to see in the dark. We passed trailers and motor homes, little pop-top campers, and tents of all kinds, one right after another. There were what looked like Christmas-tree lights strung on the canopies of some trailers and colored plastic lanterns on others. It was like a little city.

We went all the way around the area designated for motor homes twice before we finally found our little post, and then Dad had sort of a rough time getting into it just right, because it wasn't what they call a "drive-through." He had to back in. Some motor homes have TV cameras on the back and monitors over the dashboard so the driver can see to back up, but not *Brunhilda*. All she has is two enormous mirrors. Three times he tried, and three times he had to stop suddenly to keep from hitting the motor home in site 17-A. He had to send Ben out with flashlights to guide him—like those guys at airports. Finally, though, he got us in—a little crooked, but not bad for the first time. We all cheered and clapped and stamped our feet.

We were there. At our first campground, in our first campsite. Our first night in *Brunhilda* was about to begin.

.... Home, Sweet Home ....

Dad went out to plug us in and attach us to the water line. Ben disappeared with his two flashlights, presumably to explore the campground. One minute he was there, the next he was gone. Rick found another flashlight and, after warnings from Mom about talking to strangers and wandering too far, went to see if he could find any wild animals. Marcia got the leash and took Buffy for a walk. I was left to help Mom with dinner.

"What're we having?"

Mom had set the largest of the camping cook pots on the stove and was crouched in the aisle between the table and the sink, looking through the cans in the slide-out pantry. "Chili. I made it at home, so all we need to do is heat it up. Also canned fruit, if I can find where I put it. Get the chili out of the fridge, would you? It's in the big plastic container."

I stood there, waiting for her to find what she was looking for and stand up again so I could get by. After a moment, she looked over her shoulder. "Now, Jenny. Everybody's starved."

"I can't get by."

She looked at her position, back at me, and got up. "Sorry. This is going to take some getting used to." I still couldn't get by. She slid the pantry back in and then had to lean up

54

against the sink so I could squeeze past. Then she went back to searching the pantry, which is why she wasn't looking when I opened the refrigerator.

It could have been worse. Even right then, I knew it could have been worse. I might have been barefoot. As it was, at least there wasn't any blood.

I had to tug to get the refrigerator door open because all the catches to all the doors were very tight, so they wouldn't pop open while we were on the road. It didn't open, so I tugged harder. Then it was as if someone had thrown a grenade. A food grenade. The door flew open and everything from inside hurled itself out at me. Jars of ketchup and mayonnaise, mustard and pickles and salad dressing crashed into my legs, into each other, and onto the floor, where they broke. The chili, in its plastic container with the magic seal, aimed for my stomach, missed, and cracked me in the knees on its way down. The magic seal let go. Two half-gallon cartons of milk from the top shelf had the farthest to fall. Amazingly, one of them didn't break open when it hit the rubble beneath.

The refrigerator was almost empty. A carton of eggs had caught on the front ledge of the shelf and was balanced precariously like a seesaw, six of its twelve egg cups dangling in midair. A head of lettuce had rolled forward, but changed its mind and stopped just before plunging over the edge.

I said there was no blood; I didn't say there was no pain. The mayonnaise and pickle jars had landed on my left foot just before they shattered against each other. I suspected broken toes. From the floor to my knees, I was covered with chili, milk, pickle juice, and mustard. Luckily for Mom, she'd had the pantry out again. It had acted like a shield so that it was liberally spattered, but she was unscathed.

Later we were to discover that refrigerators aren't the only dangerous storage areas in a motor home—they're just the ones with the messiest contents. When you've been on the road, you have to open every door carefully because things leap out. A moving motor home is sort of like a house, but it's a house surviving a continual earthquake.

There is no point disgusting you with the full details of the half hour that followed. But you should remember that *Brunhilda* has shag carpeting. It isn't easy to get bits of broken glass out of shag carpeting. We couldn't even use the vacuum cleaner, because everything was too wet, partly from the food and partly from the gallons of water it took to get rid of the stickiness.

When we'd gotten as much of the mess cleaned up as we could, and I'd changed clothes, I took the garbage bag full of gunk and broken glass out to 18-A's trash can, leaving Mom alone to figure out what to do about dinner. None of the rest of the family had come back yet—not even Dad, who'd only gone out to get us hooked up. I stayed outside to breathe the fresh air and to catch everybody as they came back and tell them what had happened before they started asking stupid questions. Dinner was likely to be strained enough as it was.

We ate what was left—scrambled eggs, canned green beans, lettuce without dressing, and bread. We had very small glasses of milk to drink. Dad comforted Mom by reminding her that the park had a store where we could replace everything we'd lost except the chili. She was a good sport about it, but I had a feeling she wasn't quite as fond of *Brunhilda* right then as she'd been at first. My toes still hurt, and I knew one thing for sure. I wasn't ever going to be the first one to open the refrigerator again.

There isn't enough room at the dinette for all six of us to eat there, so Mom and Dad sat in the living room and used the table between the swivel chairs. The four of us kids used the dinette, and even so, it was really crowded. Rick kept complaining that Ben was purposely jabbing him with his elbow. (But Rick doesn't like scrambled eggs for breakfast, let alone for dinner, so he was pretty crabby anyway.)

After dinner, Dad told Ben and Marcia to do the dishes. With them in the galley, nobody could get through, so I went back to the bedroom, turned on the light, and closed the door. It was cozy and private that way. I planned to write a letter to Sarah.

The cats were still in their carriers on Marcia's bed. Chatter hadn't given up the idea that she could make the air holes big enough to get out of. All the holes were ragged with claw marks, and she was still working at it. She was also still meowing, though not as loudly. She seemed to be getting hoarse. I opened the carrier to let her out, and she was so surprised, she just stood there for a minute, blinking her blue, slightly crossed eyes. I opened Czar Nicholas's carrier, too, but he was lying flat on his back, his paws draped across his chest, snoring slightly. He didn't stir a whisker.

Once Chatter realized she was free, she jumped out, circled the bed twice, then leaped over to my bed and circled it, too. Then she tested the curtains for climbing, jumped from there down to the floor, and began pacing, her tail straight in the air. She also started meowing again, and as clearly as if she'd used the words, I knew what she wanted.

"Where's the litter box?" I called.

Nobody heard, so I went to open the door and Ben shouted that he was using the bathroom.

"Where's the litter box?"

"How should I know?"

"Can't you shut yourself in the side with the john and let me through? I need to find the litter box."

"I'll only be a minute."

"I'm not sure I have a minute. Ask somebody about the litter box!"

Nobody remembered packing the litter box. Mom remembered putting it out, along with the bag of litter, the cat chow, and the food bowls, but nobody remembered packing any of those things. In fact, nobody remembered seeing them. We found Buffy's tie-out chain, the dog chow, and her dishes in one of the outside storage compartments. We also found a box full of She-Ra princess dolls no one had seen before.

"Crumb-grabber toys," Dad said.

But there was nothing for the cats.

"Nobody loves the cats!" Rick wailed. "Nobody cares!"

"Don't be silly." Mom's voice took on her cheerful-but-determined tone. "We all care. However it happened, it happened. Now, who knows what we can use for a litter box?"

Rick thought we could just pile some sand on the floor in a corner of the back bedroom. Marcia and I vetoed that. Finally, we had to use the frying pan.

"I won't eat anything that's been cooked in that ever again," Ben said.

"That's fine. As far as I'm concerned, we can eat every

meal at a restaurant for the duration of the trip!" Mom's
cheerful tone was slipping.

Dad jumped in quickly. "Ben was just joking," he assured
her. "A little boiling water and some Lysol and it'll be good
as new."

Ben was sent, protesting, to get some sand from the
campground's swimming beach.

When he got back, we had to figure out where to put the
pan. Everybody but Marcia and me wanted it in our bedroom. Finally, since the bathroom had the only floor space
that didn't have to be used all the time, we put it in front
of the toilet, where it would have to be moved out into the
hall every time anybody needed the facilities. Chatter didn't
even seem to notice the unusual shape of the pan or the
texture of the litter. The minute we put it down she jumped
in, and I could swear I heard her sigh with relief. We retired
to the front room to give her some privacy.

Then Dad attached Buffy's chain outside and, ignoring
Rick's protests, put her out on it with her food and water
dish. It's amazing how much space an almost golden retriever can take up. Everybody but Rick was glad to have
her out from under foot. He kept complaining about it until
Dad promised that she could come in to sleep or if it started
to rain.

When the dishes were all done and put away, it was
nearly eleven, but nobody was ready to go to bed. It was
our first night in *Brunhilda,* and we wanted to sit around
and appreciate how comfortable we were, compared to
being crowded into a tent on air mattresses. So we decided
to watch television for a while, except for Ben, who went
back to Marcia's and my room to read. Dad turned the TV

set on. Snow. He switched channels. Snow and static. Once, just after he switched to a new channel, there was a minute or so when, looking very carefully, you could make out some shapes—it looked like a car chase through a blizzard—and then they were gone. On one channel we got music and some people talking, but you couldn't make out what they were saying through the static. When he'd been through all the channels, both VHF and UHF, twice, he turned it off. "Must be a bad location," he said.

"Or a bad television," Rick said.

"Or a bad antenna," Marcia said.

"Oh, well, who needs television on vacation anyway?" Mom asked.

"I do." This was Rick again.

"Tough." Mom had not had a great day.

For that matter, none of us had. So when Dad suggested turning in, nobody protested. Tomorrow we could all start fresh.

"First dibs on the shower," I said. I still felt sticky all over from the chili.

Since Rick had to brush his teeth and use the toilet, we were going to have a chance to see how the split bathroom worked. I evicted Ben from our room, got undressed, put on my robe, and went to the tub/shower room. It's an exaggeration to call it a room. Once you close the door you are *in* the tub. I had to stand in it, take off my robe, and drop it and my towel outside. Then I turned on the water. It didn't exactly "shower" down. It sort of spurted and sort of dribbled. I decided to think of it as gentle. When it got hot, I stood very close and it felt good. Very good. It was hot and wet, and the small space got steamed up very quickly. The nice thing about the gentle spray was that I didn't have to worry about getting my hair wet. If I'd wanted to, I could have taken the nozzle down and sprayed it directly on my hair. As it was, I could keep my head well out of the way. I just stood there, letting all the stresses of the day run off me with the hot water. It was wonderful. A long, comforting, wonderful shower. I love showers. Hot. Hot. Hot. Warm. Not so warm. Cool. Cold!

"Hey," I yelled. "Who's running the hot water?"

"Nobody," Marcia called from our bedroom.

"Well, somebody must be doing something!" I turned off the freezing water, but it was too late. I wasn't warm anymore—I was shivering. Even the steam was gone. I cracked the door and got my towel—it was even colder out there—and I dried myself as well as I could, bumping my elbows into the walls and the door. Then I traded the towel for my robe, put it on, and went out into the living room.

"What happened to the hot water?" I demanded.

"What do you mean, what happened to it?" Mom asked. She was folding Rick's clothes onto one of the swivel chairs. Rick, in his pajamas, was already tucked into his bunk.

"It's all gone."

Dad, who had been up on the roof getting Ben's sleeping bag out of one of the clamshells, where he'd packed it, forgetting that Ben would need it every night, came back inside.

"What's gone?"

"The hot water."

"Did you use it all up?"

I shook my head. "I couldn't have. I was only halfway through my shower when all of a sudden it was gone. I didn't even wash my hair."

"Did you run the water the whole time?" Dad asked.

There was accusation in his voice.

"Of course I did. I was taking a shower!"

"The water heater only holds six gallons, Jenny."

I thought about that. Six gallons. Most fish tanks hold more than six gallons. "Well, how is anybody supposed to take a shower with six gallons of hot water?"

"You turn on the water and get yourself wet. Then you turn off the water, soap down, turn on the water, and rinse off. Period."

"That's not a shower!"

Dad raised his voice so everyone would hear. "Shower rule number one: No continuous running of water. Rule number two: No showers will take more than three minutes."

"But what if I have to wash my hair?"

"Same principle. Wet your hair, turn off the water and shampoo it, turn on and rinse."

"Gross. Just gross."

I'd have said more, but I suddenly remembered the campground showers we'd had to use one time when we went tent camping. There had been a meter in every shower stall, and you had to put in a quarter to start the water at all. Then, halfway through shampooing, it would stop, and you had to put in another quarter. At least in *Brunhilda* it was free.

"What about my shower?" Marcia asked.

"Tomorrow," Mom said. "Unless you want it cold."

"Tomorrow," Marcia agreed.

"I won't use up the water," Rick said. "I won't take showers."

"Gross, gross," I said, and went to brush my teeth.

Mom and Dad pulled the bed out from the couch. It was

supposed to be a double bed, but it sure didn't look like one. When they both got in, they were squished like sardines in a can. And Mom would have to climb over Dad if she had to get up in the night. The bed took up so much room there was no place for Buffy to sleep except in front of the sink. Ben's bed, which was made by taking the pedestal out from under the dinette table and lowering it onto the benches, then rearranging the cushions so they covered the whole area, was just right for him if he lay sort of crossways in it. It, too, was billed as a double. Maybe two people Rick's size could have managed. Marcia and I were lucky. We had real beds in a real room.

When I got into my bed, with the comatose Czar Nicholas stretched out next to my legs (Chatter was still hyped on tranquilizer and still pacing, but quietly now) and my very own pillow fluffed up under my head, all I needed was Foof standing next to the bed and I'd have felt completely at home (except for a few lumps under me, where the jeans and shorts had bunched up a little). The back air conditioner was humming gently, I was snug and sleepy, Marcia was less than two feet away, and there was something friendly and comfortable about having the whole family going to bed at the same time, so close together. We did a sort of Walton family good-night, turned out the lights, and I closed my eyes. The Getaway seemed, once again, a wonderful idea.

.........Shakedown..........

It still seemed that way in the morning when the gray light of dawn crept around the slats of the blinds and the wakeup calls of about three million birds drowned out the air conditioner's hum. I woke up sort of gently and realized where we were—in the woods, away from the hustle and bustle of city life. I lay there for a while, listening to the birds, and gradually became aware of the smell of freshly perked coffee. Mom must be up, I thought. Marcia was still asleep, Czar Nicholas was still zonked on tranquilizer, and Chatter was nowhere to be seen. I felt good. It was early, but I wasn't sleepy. Just comfortable. Contented. I was going to love this vacation. It was clearly the best idea Mom and Dad had ever had.

Crash! Thump! Slam! "Get back in here, Johnny, and get your breakfast!"

"I'm gonna catch breakfast!" *Crash! Thump! Slam, whap!* Loud crying.

"I said, get back inside!" *Thump, thump! Slam!*

So came to an end the quiet, cozy dawn. Marcia sat up in bed as if she'd been hit by lightning. "What? Who? What's happening?"

I peeked out through the blinds. No woods. In front of me, less than eight feet away, was the white expanse of another motor home. Through the window I could make

64

out the gestures of an apparent fight between a very large person and a smaller one. Sobs and shouts, though muffled now, overwhelmed birds and air conditioner alike.

"Johnny wants to fish, but his mother wants him to eat first."

"What?"

"Our neighbors. Lovely people."

Clearly, the day had begun. *Brunhilda* rocked as Rick jumped out of his bunk. Ben's waking groans filled the air, Buffy barked to go out, and Chatter, pacing the dashboard, started meowing again. Two men walked by outside, mere inches from the window. They were carrying fishing equipment and arguing very loudly about whether the bait one of them had bought would work to catch anything worth eating. Another door slammed. A baby cried. "Welcome to the woods," I said, and, shoving the litter pan into the hall, closed myself into the bathroom before anybody could beat me to it.

Mom let everybody have coffee when we were up and dressed. There was just enough milk left to lighten it a bit. Ben turned his bed back into a dinette, Dad made the couch a couch again, and Rick discovered that both his and Ben's sleeping bags could be stored in his bunk when it was put back up. So it didn't take too long for *Brunhilda* to be ready for the day. Mom made pancakes with the kind of mix that needs only water. Luckily, the syrup had been in the pantry, not the refrigerator. So by seven, we were all in a pretty good mood.

"I think we should stay here, today," Dad announced over his second cup of coffee. "We'll replenish supplies at the campground's store and see what the park has to offer. What do you say?"

"But we're supposed to go on to the Adirondacks," Marcia protested.

"The point of this trip is flexibility. We made plans as guidelines, not as law."

Marcia is not big on flexibility. Marcia likes to know where she stands and what's going on—as far in advance as possible. That's a drawback to the organized mind. I, on the other hand, was grateful. I was in no hurry to jolt and bump around on the highway again. I was sure that if the refrigerator stayed in one place, things wouldn't leap out.

"Besides," Mom said, "we need some shakedown time. We need to get used to *Brunhilda*, and she needs to get used to us. Maybe a couple of days here?"

Dad shrugged. "Whatever we want. Flexibility, that's the word. Flexibility and freedom. Now, whose turn is it to do the dishes?"

Making beds has never been a priority with me. But when most of your clothes are under the bottom sheet it's a virtual impossibility. I ended up pulling the spread over everything and ignoring the lumps, but Marcia took everything down to the mattress and started over. It began to appear that compulsive neatness could be a drawback in motor-home living. On the other hand, messiness wasn't even possible. There was simply no place for the mess. I usually pile dirty clothes in a corner on the floor. There was no corner. No floor. Only the aisle between the beds. Obviously, I was going to have to learn to do things very differently.

One of the differences involved taking turns. This was for everybody. We had to take turns for the bathroom, turns making beds, turns dressing, turns fast-showering, and even turns getting from one room to another. Life in *Brunhilda* was to be resolutely Single File.

I don't mean to make it sound awful. It was lots easier than normal camping. Anyone who's ever had to dress in a tent you can't stand up in or walk a quarter of a mile to an outhouse in the middle of the night, or carry a pail with enough water to wash dishes for a family of six, would recognize the luxury we were dealing with. It's just that the "home" in "motor home" isn't quite the same as the one in "Home, Sweet. . . ."

That first full day turned out okay. Mom and Dad went to the campground store and came back with everything we needed. They'd even found a litter box and litter. They'd also had a very long talk with the people who ran the store, and were loaded with camping conveniences and handy hints. There were spring-loaded rods that fit across the refrigerator shelves to keep things from flying out, and a million plastic containers of varying sizes. The first handy hint was, "Never carry glass." Everything that couldn't be bought in plastic in the first place got put into a plastic container before storing.

Rick found a bulletin board near the main lodge that listed all the park activities for the day. One was a talk about local wildlife, to be given by a ranger and illustrated with real live captive specimens. Naturally, Rick went. By lunchtime he had found his future career, a Hero (large, two-legged, and wearing a dark green uniform), and several close friends (small, four-legged, and wearing fur).

Ben disappeared again. One minute he was sitting in the living room reading the book he'd been carrying everywhere, and the next he was gone. Marcia discovered the park's education building, complete with library, which contained not only a regular encyclopedia, but also one about animals, one about birds, and several others about

plants, flowers, insects, trees, and rocks. Marcia wasn't
going to hang around in the woods without knowing anything about them.

My discovery was the lake with its beautiful, sandy beach.
I had a tan to work on. I took my stationery (for writing
Sarah and Jason), my Walkman, my book, and my sun-
glasses and spent all morning pretending not to notice the
boys.

At lunchtime we all gathered back in *Brunhilda* for sandwiches. We had them on paper plates, with paper cups for
our drinks. We were learning.

"What's the camp store like?" Ben asked over the cookies
that were dessert.

"Why?"

Ben shrugged, as if the subject held practically no interest for him. "Oh, I just wondered. They have a lot of
stuff?"

"That depends," Mom said. "There's groceries and camping supplies, mostly."

"What kinds of camping supplies?"

"Oh, you know, canteens and folding cups and tent
stakes and insect repellent. The usual. But it's expensive.
If you think of things we need, we should stop at a discount
store when we leave here. You need anything in particular?"

Ben got that look he gets—as if he's pulling a blind down
over his face. "No. Just some stuff."

Good old communicative Ben.

"Anybody want to take a hike with me this afternoon?"
Mom asked.

I looked out the window, where the large woman from
the motor home next door was hanging laundry on a line

stretched from a tree to her side-view mirror, and hoped somebody else would volunteer. I hadn't ignored the boys at all. It was the beach for me.

"I'm going to help Harvey," Rick said.

"Who's Harvey?"

"The ranger. He's teaching me. He says I can be a Junior Ranger and have a badge and do real work for him. I'm going to clean the cages and runs this afternoon."

"Sounds fun," Ben muttered. "Excuse me." He squeezed past me into the aisle and headed for the door. "I'm going fishing."

"I'll hike, Mom." Count on Marcia. She's a good kid.

"Great. We'll get some things for dinner."

"We're hiking to a grocery?"

"Wild things, Marcia. Wild things."

"Not wild animals!" Rick yelled. "We're not eating rabbits or squirrels or anything!" You'd have thought she'd suggested cannibalism.

"Plants, Rick, not animals. Roots, leaves, berries, flowers."

"For dinner?" This was Dad. His tone was the same as Rick's.

"You'll see," Mom said. "It'll be great."

"Sure." He did not sound convinced. For Dad this trip was to meet people, not to live off the land.

"How about you, Jenny?"

"Oh, I thought I'd write Jason. Read a little. Maybe swim." I said this very casually.

"Don't get too much sun."

"I won't." As if you could get a breathtaking tan without the sun.

Dad stood up. *Brunhilda*'s ceiling was half an inch higher

than his head, but he always stooped, slightly, just in case. "I think I'll go introduce myself and get to know some of our neighbors. There are license plates here from all over."

"Yeah." This was Marcia. "But you won't have to waste a lot of time with introductions. Most people have wooden signs on their campers with all their names and where they're from. You can just go up and say, 'Hi, Harry Hennessey from Ashtabula, and how are Howie, Herkimer, and Henrietta?' "

"That's just a sign of how friendly these people are. I think of them as the Camping Fraternity," Dad said. "Real people. Nice people. With interests in common."

I thought of the yelling at dawn. Johnny's mother was real, all right. But nice? I'd only been at the campsite a few minutes all morning, and I'd heard her hit that kid at least two more times. Practically all she did was yell. Maybe it was Johnny who wasn't nice, and his mother just lacked patience. Whatever, I couldn't imagine Dad having much in common with those particular members of the Camping Fraternity. But maybe they weren't typical. One thing I knew, some of the boys at the beach were cute. Very cute.

One of them, a blond with brown eyes and a tan he must have been working on for weeks, came over to talk to me about halfway through the afternoon and bought me a Coke. Somehow I forgot to write Sarah. Or Jason. When Brad (that was his name) walked me back to *Brunhilda* at suppertime, I felt a little guilty, but not very.

Mom and Marcia were fixing dinner when I got back. At least that's what they said they were doing. It looked to me as if they were sorting the contents of a lawn-mower bag. There were weeds all over the dinette table and filling both sinks.

"We're not going to actually *eat* any of that stuff, are we?"

"Of course we are," Mom said. "I'm writing a column on edible wild plants."

"Can't you just write about them? Do we have to try them out?"

Mom was adamant. She couldn't write a column advising people to eat anything she hadn't tried herself. And since it was for the Sunday paper, in the family section, she wanted to see how the whole family liked the recipes.

That's how some of us ate dandelion greens and cattail roots (excuse me, *tubers*), and milkweed for dinner that night. I should say "with" dinner, because we also had cube steaks and tomatoes. We didn't need to worry about spoiling our appetites for those, with vast quantities of cooked weed. For one thing, the leafy stuff cooked down so much that the great batches they'd started with ended up as smallish lumps of spinachy green. I hated the dandelion greens. The milkweed was a little mushy and didn't have much taste, but it wasn't too bad, and we did reasonably well with the cattails, once Mom poured lots of melted butter over them and salted them a lot. Put enough butter and salt on something and it reminds you of popcorn, no matter what it tastes like.

Rick, who thinks broccoli and green beans are a subversive plot against the youth of America, didn't put a bite of any of it into his mouth. Dad did his duty by trying everything, and Mom smiled a lot, but I noticed she didn't eat very much of it either. Marcia actually seemed to like it all, but Ben was the one who surprised me the most. He not only ate everything, but also took seconds. He made a face at the dandelion greens, but then he asked how to cook them. And everything else. I didn't care to know. It wasn't something I ever intended to do.

Over the next few days, our "free and flexible" lives got carefully scheduled. We had to know who would fix dinner, because there wasn't room for more than one person in the galley at a time. There were signup sheets for showers and shampoos, and Dad put a big reminder on both bathrooms about the time limit.

We got very good at stepping over cats, and since Dad insisted that Buffy live outside all day every day, we only had to worry about stepping on her at night. Of course, Dad (who gets up to go to the bathroom in the middle of the night every night) managed to step on her every time. We got used to incorporating a dog yelp and a string of curses into our dreams. It was harder to sleep through Rick's occasional nighttime journey, since it began with his jumping out of his bunk, which was not only very loud, but set *Brunhilda* rocking like a tidal wave.

I spent most of the shakedown time at the beach with Brad. And, yes, I got sunburned. I started to use the sun block because Marcia said I'd have skin cancer by the time I was twenty. Also because it was nice to have Brad rub it on my back. There were lots of kids around the park—and it wasn't at all like school, where groups work at keeping other kids out. When you're camping, you move around so much that you have to make friends fast. Almost everybody who wanted to be part of a group was welcome.

We didn't do much that was useful or even exciting. We played volleyball and Frisbee. Some of the kids entered the park contests, like horseshoe pitching (Brad was really good at that) and canoe races. In one canoe race you had to paddle across the lake and back, but halfway back you had to capsize your canoe, turn it back over and get in, and paddle it back all full of water. I'd never paddled a canoe before, so even with Brad as my partner, we came in last. I kept doing everything backward.

Harvey the ranger practically adopted Rick. He told Mom and Dad that Rick had a way with animals like nothing he'd ever seen before. He let Rick do all the handling at his nature talks, including the injured fox they were hoping would get well enough to return to the wild. The fox was Rick's favorite, except for the chipmunks, who reminded him of Justin and Nicodemus. Harvey called them "rats in striped pajamas." He gave Rick a real badge and even a ranger's hat to wear. Rick was practically beside himself over that hat. He even slept in it.

Mom and Marcia tried a different wild food every night, and Mom began experimenting with sauces for them. She said it was for the column she was writing, "The Backyard Gourmet," but I noticed that the sauces she made had very powerful flavors of their own, and I didn't think it was only us she was trying to fool. Marcia, however, was a purist. She thought it was wonderful that you could just go out and pick stuff for free and eat it, so she didn't want to use lots of ingredients that had to be bought. Most of the stuff she fixed was weeds. Really weeds. Like thistles. Marcia says you can eat every single species of thistle in the world. All you have to do is wear gloves to pick them and put them in boiling water to soften the prickers so you don't get stuck when you eat them. I hated the whole idea. Anyway, there might be a poisonous thistle the scientists haven't found yet—why take a chance?

Marcia loves Projects. The wild foods got to be nearly an obsession. She collected leaves and pressed them and wrote detailed descriptions of the plants so anybody could recognize them. She put recipes with the descriptions and made a notebook she figured would get her extra credit in something at school next year. If not science, then home ec or even English. In spite of getting almost all A's, Marcia's a fanatic for extra credit. So she spent all her time gathering or cooking or taking notes or reading about weeds.

After she finished writing "The Backyard Gourmet," Mom branched out. She did a column about how to buy and pack a backpack and another about getting in shape for taking long backpacking trips. This she tried out on the beach kids—and me. She convinced Brad and a few others that it would be terrific to go on a full-day hike, so naturally I had to go along. In the column she warned people to break their hiking boots in slowly, to avoid getting blisters. They were my blisters she was talking about. She also warned them about using a backpack when you have a sunburn. After that day I refused to have anything more to do with her columns, including the apparently innocent one about the wildflowers of northern Pennsylvania. I figured with Mom even a wildflower hunt could hurt.

None of us saw a whole lot of Ben, though Marcia pointed out once that when we did see him, he always had that book. It seemed to have grown to the back pocket of his jeans. Harvey saw him once at another ranger's "Wilderness Survival" talk, but mostly Ben was visible only at meals and at bedtime.

Dad spent his time getting to know the Camping Fraternity. The first couple of days he'd come back for dinner with stories about other people's camping experiences, and it was fun listening to them—as long as we didn't have to live through them. Some people had been chased by bears at Yellowstone or nearly washed away when they were river rafting. There were stories about storms and wild animals and kids getting lost, about poison ivy and insects and even the danger of eating wild mushrooms. I was glad we had *Brunhilda* and that Mom had forbidden any eating of mushrooms, no matter how many books Marcia read about them.

Then one evening Dad came home without a single story. In fact, he didn't say a word all through dinner; he just sat there looking like Ben at his sullen worst. We were just about finished eating when there was a knock at the door, and Dad jumped as if a firecracker had gone off under his chair. He went outside, where we could hear his voice and another but couldn't tell what they were saying. Finally he came in.

"Well?" Mom said. "Are you going to tell us or not?"

Dad sighed, twiddled his mustache, and then sat down on the couch. "So much for the Camping Fraternity," he said.

Then he told us about his day. He'd been invited to go into the mountains with some of the men he'd gotten to know. He thought they were planning to fish or hike or something—some macho wilderness activity. But they didn't go on foot; they went in Jeeps and on ATVs (those all-terrain vehicles) and they took along plenty of beer. They'd gone down a dirt road until they came to where a chain with a sign prohibiting motorized vehicles was stretched between two posts. One of the men cut the chain, and they went on till they reached a clearing where they parked and got out their coolers. Then they'd spent the rest

of the afternoon drinking beer and tossing the empty cans
into the bushes, roaring around the woods on their ATVs,
and shooting at birds and squirrels with pellet guns.

"Birds and squirrels!" Rick squealed.

"Never mind, they never hit any. I'd have left, but I had
no idea where we were. I just had to wait till they were
ready to come back. That was the head ranger just now,
wanting some more information. I made a complaint."

"Good for you!" Rick said.

After the dishes were done, Dad got out all his maps and
guidebooks and spread them over the dinette table. He said
it was time we moved on, and he was looking for a small
town where we could set up camp on the village green. He
wanted to find a place we could get to before dark if we
left by noon the next day. Rick didn't want to leave Harvey
and the animals, and Ben got one of his grumpy, sullen
looks. But I didn't really mind leaving. I'd been spending
an awful lot of time with Brad, and there's just so much
talk about fishing and hunting and football I can stand.
Anyway, I suspected Brad was going to grow up to fit right
in to the Camping Fraternity Dad had described.

When Brad came by and asked if I wanted to go to the
dance at the rec hall, I agreed. It would be a chance to say
good-bye. The thing was, even if I didn't want to spend the
rest of my natural life with him, he was gorgeous and I
liked the way he danced. Later, when he walked me back,
I also liked the way he kissed. But then Ben arrived, climbed
onto *Brunhilda*'s roof, and started rummaging around in
the clamshells. We said good-bye and Brad left. I went
inside, feeling very glad we'd come to this particular park.

Rick was in his bunk, Mom and Dad were playing cards,
and Marcia was asleep with Chatter and Czar Nicholas

curled up in the crook of her legs. I was about to use the bathroom when Ben pushed past me and got in first. I grumped at him, but Mom reminded me that Ben doesn't take long to get ready for bed—he must spend all of three seconds brushing his teeth—and sure enough, he was back out in no time. He changed the dinette into his bunk and was in his sleeping bag by the time I came out.

"G'night," he said.

It was to be the last thing any of us heard Ben say for quite a while, but since we didn't know that, everyone who was still awake just said good-night back.

.... Ben Goes It Alone ....

The next morning, when the neighbors woke us as usual with a screaming fight, Ben was gone. This wasn't, by itself, unusual. He'd been going off early in the morning nearly every day. What was unusual was the note in the middle of the dinette table. Mom found it when she went to put the coffee on. It said,

> I've gone to "my side of the mountain," like Sam Gribley. I don't think you could find me, but please don't come looking. Sorry, Dad, but I already had this all planned. I thought we were staying longer. Be back in a couple of days. DON'T SEND THE RANGERS! Love, Ben.

Well, the first thing that happened after Mom shrieked and then read the note out loud to all of us, was that Dad had a fit. A real fit.

"How could he do that?" he yelled. "How could he just take off like that, when he knew I wanted to leave today? How could he be so irresponsible? How could he ignore somebody else's wishes like that?"

Marcia said, "Maybe he thought you ignored his wishes when you planned this trip," and I held my breath. I was thinking the same thing but didn't dare say it out loud. But Dad didn't even seem to notice the interruption.

"We'll have to find him. And if we can't, the rangers will. And who's this Sam Gribley?"

"The boy in *My Side of the Mountain*," Mom said.

"And what, exactly, is 'my side of the mountain'?"

"The book he's been carrying everywhere. I gave it to him."

"You gave it to him? Does that mean you're responsible for this nonsense?"

"I didn't know he would try to copy the kid. I only knew I had to do something. He didn't want to come on this trip, you know. He didn't want to leave those computer fantasy games."

"Yes, but he got over that."

"What do you think changed his mind? Magic? Your talk about real people? It was that book, Michael. It seemed to me that if he thought this trip could be as exciting as his imaginary caves and dungeons, he'd want to come. It worked."

"Exactly what is this book about?"

"It's the story of a boy who leaves home and goes into the mountains to live on his own. He lives in a tree."

"Like a chimpanzee?" Rick asked.

"No. Inside the trunk."

"Like Winnie the Pooh!"

Mom nodded. "Exactly. He burns the trunk out the way Indians used to burn out logs to make canoes. And then he lives inside."

"And you think Ben has been burning out trees in the state park? We'll all be jailed." Dad's face was turning pinker by the minute.

"Is the book a true story?" Marcia asked.

"No. It's fiction. But I'm not sure Ben knows that."

"Has our son been burning trees in a state park?" Dad asked again. He seemed to be fixated on that idea.

"I'm sure not. Sam Gribley built a lean-to at first. That's probably what Ben's planning. Listen, even though the book is fiction, the survival information in it isn't. The author knows a lot about living in the wild."

"Does the book say what to do about bears?" Rick asked. "What if a bear comes?"

"There aren't any bears here," Dad said.

"Yes, yes, yes, there are," Rick said. "People don't see them very often, because there aren't a lot of them, but there are bears. Harvey said so. There are."

"It doesn't matter whether there are or not, because Ben is not staying out there alone. We'll get the rangers out to find him." Dad's face hadn't lightened up any.

"But he doesn't want you to do that," I said.

"He's a fourteen-year-old and I'm his father and I say we're getting the rangers to find him and then we are leaving here exactly as I've planned!"

Mom put her hand on Dad's arm. "Michael, remember the whole point of this trip—flexibility. You can hardly claim flexibility for you and not for anybody else."

Dad made a face, but you could tell he was defeated by that one. "All right, but we'll have to call the rangers anyway. It isn't safe for him to be out there alone."

Mom frowned. "That worries me, too. He hasn't any experience. All he's got is that book."

"And there are bears!" Rick said.

I had one of my dreadful visions. In it there was this dark, shadowy figure wearing a ski mask and carrying this gigantic machete through the trails of the park, ready to chop to pieces anybody he found out there alone. "It isn't bears

I'd worry about," I said. "It's slashers."

"Slashers?"

"You know, like *Friday the Thirteenth*."

"Don't be silly," Mom said. "And, anyway, how do you know about movies like *Friday the Thirteenth*?"

Caught. I smiled innocently. "I've just heard about them. All the kids talk about them." She didn't need to know what Sarah and I watch on their cable movie channel.

She didn't care about movies right then. "I don't think we have to worry about bears *or* slashers. But he could definitely get lost out there. We're right on the edge of a national forest here. There are miles and miles of woods."

"And rangers who know every inch of it," Dad said. "We're not in the wilds of Borneo. We're in Pennsylvania, for heaven's sake, Ellie. The worst danger is probably poison ivy. It's everywhere. He'll probably sleep right in the middle of a patch of it and have to spend the whole rest of this trip wrapped up in bandages and embalmed in calamine lotion. We'll spend the whole summer with a mummy."

"It just isn't fair to sic the rangers on him," Mom said. "At least not yet. He's doing this to prove something, Michael. Don't you remember what it was like to be fourteen? Don't you remember adolescence? It's all about finding out who you are and then proving it to yourself and everybody else."

Dad drew himself up. "Don't be silly. I didn't have to prove who I was when I was that age. I knew then and I know now."

Mom didn't even answer that. "No, Michael, it definitely wouldn't be right to mount a search." She looked out between the slats of the blinds at the sky. "The weather looks all right. I'm almost sure he'll be okay today."

"Will he come home to sleep?" Rick asked.

"I doubt it," Mom said. "It wouldn't be proving much if he just stayed out for the day."

"A bear'll get him in the night!"

"Or a slasher . . ."

"Hush, Jenny." Mom ran water into the coffeepot. "We'll give him till tomorrow."

"I'm going to call the rangers," Dad said.

Mom started to shake her head, then stopped. "All right, we can tell them what he's doing, but we aren't going to send them after him. If they think there's a problem, they'll tell us. Otherwise, let's let him try this. After all, Michael, I spent two weeks alone in a *real* wilderness area when I was a kid."

"You were eighteen, you'd had plenty of experience, and you weren't destroying someone else's plans at the time."

"Flexibility, Michael." By the look on Dad's face, I could tell he wished he'd never used that word.

"There's probably nothing to worry about," Harvey told Dad later that morning. "A reasonably bright fourteen-year-old who knows something about survival ought to be all right for a day or two."

"What about bears?"

"He's not likely to run into a bear, Rick. And even if he did, the bear would probably be more frightened than Ben. Do you know what equipment he took?"

Mom shrugged. "He's got one of the frame packs, his sleeping bag, probably a knife, and some fishing gear."

"A compass?"

Marcia had been sent to pick up a loaf of bread at the

campground store, and she got back at this point. "I asked the woman at the store if she'd seen him. She says Ben's been there a whole bunch of times in the last couple of days, asking questions and buying things. He bought a flint and steel—"

"What's that?" Rick asked.

"It's for making fires," Harvey said. "They keep them at the store as souvenirs more than anything. Nobody uses them anymore."

"Sam Gribley used flint and steel instead of carrying matches," Mom said.

"Sam?"

"Never mind," Dad said. "What else did he buy, Marcia?"

"A compass and some fishing line, one of those hatchets with the holster thing that goes on your belt, a canteen, and a mess kit—you know, the kind that has a little frying pan and a plate and cup and fork."

"Any food?" This was Mom.

"Nope. He asked about drinking water and good fishing spots, and he asked about trails into the real wilderness."

"Wonderful," Dad grumbled. "It'll take forever to find him."

Harvey patted Rick's head. "Come on, Junior Ranger, we've got a wildlife program in fifteen minutes." He looked from Dad to Mom and back again. "Don't worry about your son, folks. We'll keep an eye out for him. But if he knows how to make a fire and catch fish, he'll be okay. I'd be willing to bet he'll be back tomorrow morning after he's proved to himself he can stay out alone all night. If it rains, he'll be back even sooner. If you want, we'll start a real search, but I don't think it'll be necessary."

Mom shook her head. "I'd rather give him time to come back on his own. But I feel better knowing you're aware he's out there."

"We'll probably know exactly where he is if he gets a fire going. Somebody's bound to see the smoke. Luckily we've had a wet spring, so he isn't likely to start a forest fire or anything."

"You mean Ben could start a fire like in *Bambi*?" Rick asked, his eyes round and horrified.

Harvey laughed. "Unless he took matches along, too, he'll be lucky to get a campfire going, let alone a forest fire. Flint and steel are the dickens to use if you don't know how."

So Harvey and Rick went off to teach people about porcupines and chipmunks, Marcia took the field guide to edible wild plants and went off to see if she could find groundnuts, Mom set up her typewriter to work on her next column, and Dad took a book called *Blue Highways* and settled on the couch to read—or sulk. I went to find Brad. It was obvious we were going to have another day here at least.

Teenaged boys, especially gorgeous ones with good tans, are a fickle lot. Brad hadn't wasted so much as one morning pining over me. By the time I got down to the beach, he was with a girl with very long, unreal-looking blond hair, a teeny little string bikini (way smaller than mine), and a tan as good as his. Luckily, I saw them from the parking lot and didn't get close enough to the beach for Brad to see me.

I decided I'd had enough sun. I decided that since I hadn't started to read the book I'd taken down to the beach that first day, today would be an excellent time to read it. And write Sarah again. And Jason. Nice, indoor activities

that could be—had to be—accomplished alone. Brad and
that girl, I thought on my way back to *Brunhilda,* would
be covered with terrible wrinkles by the time they were
thirty. They'd look as if they were made of leather. They'd
probably have skin cancer. I, on the other hand, would have
a light, creamy complexion and a mind enriched and en-
hanced by the reading of fine literature.

Mom was clattering away on her portable typewriter
when I got back, writing a column on the drawbacks of
going into the wilderness alone. Dad had taken Buffy for
a walk. I asked if I could read what Mom had written so
far, and for the first time in my life realized where my
tendency to visualize catastrophes comes from—I'd always
thought it was my own personal hang-up. Especially since
Mom always seems so tough. Maybe when you're a mother
you're tough for yourself and a wimp about your kids. The
first part of her column was about things like falling and
breaking a leg and lying on the ground for days with no
help, or getting wet and dying of hypothermia when a wind
came up or the air got cold at night, or eating the wrong
thing and poisoning yourself.

Of course, she didn't put in my slasher or Rick's bear,
but she did make what Ben was doing sound dumb. You'd
never have guessed, from that column, that she'd done the
same thing herself. When I pointed that out to her, she
said she'd done it properly. She'd filed plans for her trip
with a park office before she left so somebody would at least
know where to look if she didn't come back when she was
supposed to. Still, I bet she didn't think of all those awful
possibilities when she went out alone as a kid. Not only
that, where she went there were bears, all right—grizzly
bears.

"I thought you wanted us kids to get to know the wilderness."

Mom looked up from her typing. "Of course I do. But I want you to get to know it with someone who knows how to handle it."

"But you gave him the book."

"I know, I know. And if he follows it carefully, he'll probably be fine. I just hope . . ."

"What?"

"I just hope he doesn't run into any kind of trouble out there, that's all. Something the book doesn't warn him about or tell him how to handle."

"Are you really worried?"

"No. Yes. No. Jenny, I thought you were going to the beach."

"Changed my mind."

"Well, go someplace else, then. I've got to finish this column."

I can take a hint. Well, that wasn't exactly a hint, more like a hammer over the head, but I went and closed myself into Marcia's and my bedroom and tried to read my book and not think about slashers and bears and poison ivy. I tried not to think of Ben lying with one leg twisted at a sickening angle, half in and half out of a stream, slipping slowly away as the warmth and life drained out of his body.

Supper that night was hot dogs and potato chips and plums from the campground store. Marcia had tried cooking leaves of some kind, but even she couldn't manage to choke these down, they were so bitter, and Mom was in no mood to make a sauce to disguise them. It seemed weird not to have Ben eating with us, and I could tell Mom and

Dad were both getting more and more edgy. I sort of hoped
it would rain so he'd come home before morning. Partly I
wanted to leave so I didn't have to see Brad and that blond
around the park, and partly I had all those visions of Ben
in trouble out there somewhere. Rick had told me all about
the porcupine he'd handled at the wildlife program, and
how dangerous the quills could be if a dog got them in its
face and there wasn't anybody to get them out. The quills
have these barbs that let them work farther and farther in.
So now I saw Ben covered with porcupine quills that were
working their way insidiously toward his vital organs. By
the time people even started looking for him, he'd be done
for—we'd find him with a broken leg, blue from hypothermia, with quills sticking out everywhere. Stone dead.

We tried playing cards after dinner, but nobody was really
with it. Mom kept looking out as if she could see past her
reflection into the night outside, and Dad kept grumping
about the new people who'd pulled into site 17-A after the
yellers had left that morning, and who'd done nothing but
play loud music and drink beer from the moment they got
plugged in. Finally, we gave it up and went to bed, where
I had nightmares all night. In one, Jason came to the campground to find me and was attacked by a bear with a
machete.

When we woke up Ben wasn't back. Nobody said much
at breakfast. Right afterward, Dad went down to talk to the
rangers. Mom didn't tell him not to send them out looking.
There wasn't a word said about adolescence. But when Dad
got back, he was grinning.

"They know where he is!" he said. "He's built himself a
lean-to and he's not too faraway. I'll go get him and we can
get on the road. You all get packed."

"Did they talk to him?" Mom asked.

"No, they just saw that he was okay. I'll get him and be back in less than an hour."

"No," Mom said.

"What?"

"I said no."

"I know what you said. I don't know why. We can get going now. Today!"

Mom shook her head. "Michael, do we have to go through this all over again? We can't go drag him in as if he's a baby. He's fourteen."

"I wouldn't care if he were ninety-three. I want to get out of here and away from these rowdy maniacs! Besides, you were worried half to death last night, and don't try to pretend you weren't."

"Yes, but that was before we knew where he was. Now that the rangers have found him, we'll know if something happens. Meantime, we can let him finish proving whatever it is he's proving."

"How long did that kid in the book stay out?"

"Ten months." Dad started to say something, but Mom cut him off. "He's not going to stay out there for ten months. We can at least give him another day. Just one more day."

And so we stayed. The blond's family had moved on, and Brad came over to ask me to go to the beach with him, but I have my pride. I went canoeing with Marcia and Mom.

Ben appeared shortly before dinner, wearing the backpack, the hatchet, and his new, now thoroughly muddy hiking boots, looking grimy and tired but grinning triumphantly. "I did it!" he announced, as he climbed up *Brunhilda*'s stairs. "I lived on my own in the woods for thirty-six hours! I didn't even take a tent. Or matches. Or a fishing pole. I made my own fish hooks, and I made my own shelter."

"Congratulations," Mom said. She looked meaningfully at Dad, who was making hamburger patties in the galley. They must have talked about how to handle Ben's return, because Dad didn't yell or even mention the disruption of his plans.

"Right," he said. "Congratulations. Are you eating with us, O Great and Mighty Hunter?"

Ben shrugged. "I guess so. I haven't had dinner."

"Did you see any bears?" Rick asked.

"Don't be silly. There aren't any bears around here."

"Are too."

"Well, I didn't see any. These woods are too tame," Ben said, taking off the pack and dumping it on the couch. "When are we going up to the Adirondacks, where there's *real* wilderness?"

"Soon," Dad said, slapping at a meat patty. "But the next stop is going to be a village green. We're going to have a few days in a small town, where real people live the way Americans used to—no rush and bustle, no crime in the streets, friendliness, and good neighbors—it's just what—" He was interrupted by an eruption of rock music from the motor home next door. "Just what we need," he shouted over the din. He slapped a hamburger into the frying pan. "And no more cattails for dinner."

I think everybody was more than a little relieved to have Ben safely back. Rick didn't even complain about Ben's elbow in his side while we ate. Ben ate three hamburgers and drank four glasses of milk and zonked as soon as we finished and he could turn the dinette back into his bed.

..... The Village Green .....

Packing up the next morning wasn't as hard as when we
first packed at home, but it wasn't as much of a snap as
the motor-home people would have you believe, either. After
all those days in one place, *Brundilda* had become more
homelike. There were things sitting around where they
couldn't sit once we were on the road. Everything had to
be stowed away again, and we soon found out that somehow
there was more to stow than there had been before.

Rick, all by himself, had acquired practically a library of
pamphlets, a collection of dead bugs, another collection
(stored in a paper bag) of rocks with possible fossils, and
maps of all the hiking trails in the park. Dad made him
throw away the rocks, the maps and the bugs, over his loud
protests, and let him keep only the pamphlets, which he
could store under his pillow when his bunk was folded up.
Marcia had a collection of leaves that she absolutely refused
to give up because she needed them for identification of
edible plants. She'd also spent a pretty sizable portion of
her vacation money on field guides. Ben's survival items
weren't big and could fit in a clamshell. Mom and Dad and
I didn't have much that was new, which was lucky. We
discovered an amazing thing. When something is stored
neatly away, it may not take up much space, but when you
take it out and use it, something happens. It's bigger when

you try to put it back, and it won't fit anymore. Einstein should have looked into this problem—it seems to me it has to do with relativity. There's probably a law of physics that explains the expansion of belongings when removed from storage.

Worst of all was the laundry. We'd used the campground's Laundromat once, so *all* our clothes weren't dirty, but the duffel bag for laundry was still too big to fit in either clamshell, in the closet, or in the outside storage compartment. We had to stuff it under one of the swivel chairs in the living room.

At last, after a lot of crabbiness and grumping, we were ready to go. We got unplugged, Dad started the engine, and we left, rock music blaring away behind us. Leaving the campsite was much easier than getting into it, because we didn't have to do any backing. We stopped at the education center so Rick could say good-bye to Harvey and the animals. This was accompanied by tears and sobs and misery, and Harvey promised to write Rick and let him know how all the animals were doing, and whether they'd been able to release the fox back into the wild. Then we were off.

You may have noticed that so far I have hardly mentioned the cats. The thing is, they weren't very noticeable, except for the litter box in the bathroom. Mostly they slept or sat on the dinette table or the dashboard looking out. But that was while *Brunhilda* was sitting still. The minute she started moving, that changed. When *Brunhilda* moved, Chatter's fur went up and her tail puffed out. She put all four legs out, as if to brace herself, and began to meow.

"Mowr!" she said. Then, "Meeeooowwwr!" Then, "*Eeeeyyooooowwrrrrrr!*" with a sort of trill at the end. And then she started pacing. Up to the front, where she walked around Mom's feet, then jumped to Mom's lap, onto the dashboard, and back down to the floor. Then back between Marcia's and my legs (I was on the couch and Marcia was in one of the swivel chairs), up onto the back of the dinette, down to the floor, back to Marcia's and my bedroom, up on the bed, and then back to the front again, meowing and trilling the whole time.

"Who gave that cat tranquilizers?" Dad shouted.

"Nobody," Mom assured him. "She's stone-cold sober."

"Well, can't somebody shut her up? She's going to drive me crazy."

"It's not her fault," Rick yelled back. "She's scared."

"If we have an accident because my nerves have been frayed beyond bearing, it won't matter whose fault it is! Shut her up!"

Since nobody, not even Rick with his fabled way with animals, could figure out how to keep her quiet, Mom grabbed her when she made her third pass around the front, stuffed her into her carrier, and closed her into our room.

"Now, then, what's the name of this town we're looking for?" Mom asked, as she unfolded an enormous road map of New York State. We were heading north.

"Orville Corners."

"Orville Corners?"

"That's what I said." Dad was concentrating on maneuvering *Brunhilda* around a very tight curve in the road (Route 5) we'd been supposed to take coming to the park. It wasn't one whit wider or straighter than the other, which Dad had pointed out to Mom with some satisfaction.

"Where is it?" Mom asked.

"About fifty miles southwest of Adirondack Park."

Mom shook the map out and folded it, shook it out again and refolded it. "I don't see it."

"It's very small."

"What highway is it on?"

"It isn't."

"What?"

"I said, it isn't."

"What do you mean, it isn't? It has to have a highway leading to it."

"And away again," Marcia added.

"It's on a country road, not a highway. Maybe it isn't on that map."

"If it's not on this one, we're never going to find it," Mom said. "This one's as detailed as they get. How'd you find it if it isn't here?"

"I don't know. It was on one of the maps." A car came around a curve, and Dad had to swerve to the right so it could get by.

The cards Rick had spread out on the dinette table to play solitaire skidded off onto the floor. "Hey, you wrecked my game!" he yelled.

"Better than wrecking *Brunhilda*," Dad said, and glanced at Mom. "Look about an inch below Gloversville."

"Gloversville." Mom peered at the map. "Oh. There! I see it. Orville Corners. What's there? I don't see a lake or a mountain or a park or anything."

Dad sighed a sigh loud enough to be heard over *Brunhilda*'s engine. "There isn't anything at Orville Corners except Orville Corners. That's why I chose it. It has a quaint, old-fashioned sound to it. And no tourist attractions. It's just a tiny, American village. There will probably be a general store where townspeople gather. There will be a village green—maybe with a band shell or a statue of a soldier. There will probably be a white clapboard Congregational church with a steeple. And window boxes full of petunias on the houses. And a cafe with red-and-white-checked curtains and tablecloths."

I wondered where Dad had gotten this image. He hadn't ever been in Orville Corners.

"Do you know how to get there?" Mom asked.

"First star to the left and straight on till morning," Marcia muttered. I laughed. Dad didn't hear us.

"I plotted it out last night. You all just leave it to me."

And so we did. For the next two hours we meandered along on those back roads Dad liked so much. At least he liked them in theory. After half an hour he'd begun to swear at cars that came toward us in the middle of the road instead of in their own lane. Once when we got stuck behind a guy on a tractor who refused to move over and let us by, he let out a string of words none of us are allowed to use. The tractor was going all of five miles an hour.

"Think of how little gas you're using at this speed," Mom said. Dad just snarled.

We fixed sandwiches and drinks while we were stopped at a gas station—Mom still wouldn't let anybody eat while *Brunhilda* was moving—and got back on the road again, Dad still muttering at cars, curves, hills, and even once at a tree that was leaning across the road so that a limb slapped the windshield as we went underneath.

Rick, who had put away the cards after they fell off the table for the fifth time, went back to use the bathroom. When he came back, he made his way up to the front, crashing first into me and then into Marcia and stepping on Buffy's tail. He stood by Dad's shoulder without saying anything.

For a while Dad didn't pay any attention, but finally he looked around. "What are you standing there for?" he asked. "Why don't you go back and sit down?"

"Um," Rick said.

"What?"

"Nothing," Rick said. But he didn't go back.

"It can't be nothing or you'd go back and sit down. What is the matter?"

"Um—um—something's wrong with the bathroom."

"The what?"

"The bathroom."

Dad looked at Mom. "What is he talking about?"

Mom put the map down. "Rick, what are you trying to say?"

"The—um—well—I think the toilet's broken."

Mom, apparently forgetting where she was, jumped up, lost her balance, and sat back down again suddenly. "What's the matter with it?"

"It won't flush. Or—well—the blue stuff comes out all right, but it doesn't go anywhere. And now there's too much blue stuff and . . ."

Mom stood up more carefully this time, one hand on the dashboard and one on the back of her chair. "Is it overflowing?"

Rick shook his head. "It's just sitting there. Sort of sloshing around."

"Michael, stop someplace. We have to do something."

So as soon as there was a straight piece of road with enough shoulder to get off on, Dad stopped and Mom went back to the bathroom. When she came back, her face looked carved out of stone. "We didn't stop at the sanitary station before we left the park. The waste tank's full."

Dad slammed his fist into his forehead. "Why didn't you remind me, Ellie? I said last night that was the very last thing we had to do before we got on the road today."

"I forgot, Michael Skinner, and I might remind you that you did, too. Don't you put this off on me."

"So what're we going to do?" Ben asked. "Dig a latrine on the village green at Orville Corners? Or we could all use the litter box."

Dad frowned around at all of us. "Does anybody else have to go to the bathroom?" he asked.

We all shook our heads.

"Good. Because we are going on to Orville Corners, where we will ask where the nearest sanitary dumping station is. Should anyone change his or her mind, we will stop at a gas station. Is that perfectly clear?"

We all nodded.

"Good."

"Did anybody fill up the freshwater tank?" Mom asked. "We were supposed to do that this morning, too."

"No, we did not. But all we need is a hose for that. We will surely be able to do that at Orville Corners. Marcia, check the tanks."

Over the doorway there is a panel with little lights that show how full the freshwater, the gray water (from the sinks and the shower), and the wastewater (from the toilet) tanks are. Marcia went to look.

"We've only got a little fresh water, and the gray tank's almost as full as the other one."

"No one use the sinks either," Dad said.

"Drive carefully," Mom told him. "If we jolt around too much, the toilet will spill over."

So we went back onto the road, and Dad drove almost as slowly as that tractor. This time it was other drivers swearing at us. It must have been the power of suggestion; I didn't have to go to the bathroom until I found out I couldn't. And then I had to go. By the time we finally got to Orville Corners, I felt as if I were going to burst. Dad must have felt the same way because even though nobody had said a single thing, he stopped at the very first gas station.

When we were all back in *Brunhilda* and Mom had refused for the fifth time to let Rick get a Coke from the machine, Dad announced that the gas station attendant didn't know where there was a dumping station. He told us in the attendant's own words: "Youse 'ud have to try the interstate. Some a them plazas prob'ly have 'em."

"How far is the nearest interstate?" Mom asked.

"Far enough." I suspected Dad wouldn't forget to empty the waste tank ever again. Or if he forgot, Mom wouldn't.

To get to the interstate, we had to go through Orville Corners and out the other side. Right away we could tell it wasn't going to live up to Dad's description. There were no window boxes with petunias. In fact, half the houses looked as if they hadn't been painted in about fifty years. There were some two- and three-story frame houses jammed up against each other, their porches sort of leaning into one another, and there were some smaller houses—hovels would be a better word—sort of squatting in these patches of bare ground and weeds. In what you might call the "downtown" area, there were rows of storefronts, about half of which were boarded up or had their windows painted white. The ones that were still open had window displays that looked old and dusty—as if they hadn't been changed since all the houses had been painted. Dad's cafe didn't have red-and-white-checked curtains, and it didn't call itself a cafe either. It had a neon sign over its door that said EAT. That's all. Just EAT. Actually, after dark it would say E T because the glass tube for the A was broken and it didn't light up.

And there wasn't a pretty white church either. There was only a building that had once been a movie theater and now said, in hand-painted white letters across the front, THE ROCK SOLID CHRISTIAN TABERNACLE. The cross that stood on the top of the marquee was made of two big tree branches with the bark still on. Rick might have made it at day camp.

There were bars, though—one on each of the other three corners of the main intersection. I wondered how the town had enough people to keep three bars open. Their signs, each advertising a different brand of beer, weren't broken. Each one said, in red neon, BAR.

"No overstatement here," Mom said. "Eat. Bar. Direct and straightforward, these Orvillians."

"Cornerians," Ben suggested.

"Whatever."

There didn't seem to be a general store. At least not the kind Dad was talking about—with a big porch and rocking chairs and a potbellied stove inside. There was a hardware store, though. And something that actually called itself a FIVE AND DIME. It looked as if it might actually have stuff inside that only cost five cents. Or only should.

But Dad was right about one thing—the most important. Orville Corners did have a village green. One block down from the intersection with the three bars and the tabernacle, there was a kind of park. Dad was also right about the statue. It was a Union soldier standing on a marble pedestal with a brass plate on the front. Piled at each corner of the pedestal were cannonballs in a little pyramid. There was no band shell in this park, but there was grass and an attempt at a flower garden—under a straggly crab-apple tree. And there were four benches, one on each side of the park. Three of the four benches were occupied. One contained a couple of rough-looking teenage boys, cigarettes hanging from the corners of their mouths. They didn't seem to be doing anything except watching people go by on the street. The other benches contained old men, all wearing hats, including one who was dressed in an undershirt, a pair of dirty shorts, and brown leather shoes—without socks. He was playing checkers with a guy who looked as if he were dressed for a different season of the year, in long pants and a flannel shirt.

"Real people," Mom observed, as we drove by.

"Don't be judgmental, Ellie," Dad scolded. "They, too, have their story."

"Is that a quote?"

"Yes. But it's true. And I'll bet their stories are interesting."

"No doubt."

Mom didn't seem to buy this, but Marcia's eyes had taken on that shine I recognized. She had seen the possibility of an extra-credit report. She would no doubt want to take a tape recorder and ask those old men all sorts of personal questions—the way those kids did in that *Foxfire* book Dad had told us about when he was first talking about the trip.

We weren't stopping now, though. We had to find a sanitary dumping station. First things first.

But it didn't turn out to be first at all. The first service plaza on the interstate did not have a dumping station. Nor did the second. By the time we'd finally found one, we'd gone more than fifty miles beyond Orville Corners and Mom didn't want to go back. But Dad was adamant. Even seeing how different it was from his fantasy, he still wanted to spend a few days there. Like Marcia, he wanted to talk to those old men. He wanted to eat (I shuddered even thinking about it) in a place that called itself EAT and clink bottles of beer with the guys in each BAR. He probably wanted to hang around till Sunday to see what went on in THE ROCK SOLID CHRISTIAN TABERNACLE. And when Dad wants something as badly as he wanted that, who's going to argue?

So back we went, stopping at a hamburger place on the way because it was past suppertime and nobody wanted to wait till we got set up on the village green to eat. By the time we passed the chipped and peeling WELCOME TO OR-VILLE CORNERS sign and the other sign with the Rotary symbol on it, darkness had fallen. We couldn't really set ourselves up *on* the village green, of course, since it was a park and we couldn't just drive up onto the grass. The old men were gone from the bench—the teenage toughs were still there and had been joined by several more—and there were plenty of parking spaces all around the square. Dad pulled up to the curb and set the emergency brake.

"Close the blinds," Mom said. "I don't like the looks those kids are giving us."

"Don't be silly. They're just curious."

Marcia and I went around and closed all the blinds. I checked the door to be sure it was locked.

"Who's going to walk Buffy?" Rick asked.

"Your father," Mom said.

So Dad put Buffy's leash on her and went out. I noticed that he didn't take her toward the gang across the grass. And he didn't stay out long.

"Okay," he said when he came back. "Time to turn in. Tomorrow we get a taste of small-town America."

"At that EAT place?" Rick asked.

"He's speaking figuratively," Mom said. "He means we'll see what small towns are like."

"But I want to eat at EAT!"

Mom shivered, and I did, too. I'd sooner have dandelion greens.

When I got into bed, I kept thinking about those guys out there by the bench. It was silly. I mean, we were inside, our door was locked, our blinds were down, and we were as safe as if we were inside a house. But they made me very, very nervous.

Marcia was excited. "I'm going to take my tape recorder out tomorrow," she said. "I want to ask some of those old guys what this place was like when they were kids."

"Probably exactly the same as it is now," I said.

"Before cars, I mean, Jenny. When there were horses and buggies and no telephones and—

"They're not *that* old."

"Okay, but before planes and television and computers and stuff."

"From the looks of Orville Corners, it's *still* before computers."

When I turned my light out I pulled my sheet up over my head. I kept thinking of those guys outside. And you don't have to tell me it's dumb to hide under a sheet—I can't help it. I know there's nobody under my bed at home, too, but I still don't let my hand hang over the edge of the mattress, in case something's going to grab it. We all have these little quirks. Even logical, sensible Marcia. She put her sheet over her head, too.

.........Real People.........

It was light out, but just barely, when the pounding started. *Blam, blam, blam* on the door. A ten-second pause and then *blam, blam, blam.* Another pause and then *blam, blam, blam, BLAM, BLAM,* getting louder and louder. Buffy started to bark, and the noise was enough to burst eardrums. I stumbled out of bed and got to the galley, where Ben was sitting up in his bunk, rubbing his eyes, just as Dad got himself extricated from the sofa bed. He was dressed only in his underwear, so we had to listen to more pounding and barking as he pulled on a pair of shorts.

"Quiet, Buffy!" Dad said. She was standing with her nose pointed at the door, the fur over her shoulders standing straight up. "Sit!" She barked a couple more times and then sat. Dad stepped over her.

"Open up in there!" a voice shouted among the *blams.* "This is the sheriff speaking—*open up in there!*"

"What's the sheriff want?" Ben asked, and Dad shrugged as he made his way to the door. His eyes were barely open and his hair looked as if it had been stirred. He stepped down the first step, unlocked the door, and opened it a crack. It was torn out of his hand and flung wide by someone outside. I moved to see who was out there, as Marcia joined me. Buffy, seeing the open door, pushed past Dad and the guy standing outside and headed off for the grass of the village green. Luckily, Marcia had shut our door and the cats were locked in our room.

The source of all the yelling and pounding did appear to be a sheriff. He was dressed in a khaki-colored uniform and had a star-shaped badge. He was very, very tall and very, very thin. He had a crew cut and a sunburn and the longest neck I think I've ever seen on a human being— with an Adam's apple so big it looked as if he'd swallowed a tennis ball.

"What do you think you're doing here?" he asked, his voice so loud, it seemed to bounce off all the walls. He put one hand on his hip and the other—very noticeably—on the handle of the gun that stuck out of a holster at his side.

Dad started to speak, croaked, and had to clear his throat before he could find any voice at all. "We just stopped here for the night," he said.

"What do you think this is, a public campground? You can't just come into town in this disgusting vehicle and take up half the public street."

"Are we in a no-parking zone?" Dad asked. "It was dark when we got here last night, and I may have missed the sign."

"Don't screw around with me, fella. We don't want your kind in Orville Corners, parking zones or no-parking zones."

Dad ran his hand through his hair, as if that could make him more presentable. "What do you mean, 'my kind'?"

"You know exactly what I mean, you city types who think you can bring your loose morals and your filthy language and your drugs and what-all into a nice, clean American town and corrupt our kids."

Loose morals? Filthy language? Drugs? Marcia and Ben and I exchanged glances. Maybe this guy was an escaped lunatic disguised as a sheriff. If Mom hadn't been dressed only in a summer nightgown, she probably would have been out of bed and nose-to-nose with this madman. As it was, her face was about as red as the guy's sunburn. It was quite clear from Dad's back that he had taken a deep breath and was mentally counting to ten. The guy still had his hand on his gun, after all.

"I don't understand a word you've said, officer," Dad said, his voice cracking slightly. "This is a family, here—my wife and myself and our four children, and we're merely stopping—"

"Four children? You have four children in there with you?"

"Our two sons and two daughters—"

"I've heard about stuff like this, but I never thought I'd see it. Your own children! That's disgusting. What've you got in there? Marijuana? Cocaine? Heroin? I've half a mind to search you and call the state cops."

Dad's back got very straight. "Search us? Search us? That requires a warrant, I believe."

"Oh, a wise guy, huh? You been watching cop shows on TV! Well, you just see who needs a warrant here and who doesn't. This is Orville Corners, mister. A clean town in a clean county. Good, God-fearing, churchgoing people with nice, clean kids. We got no drugs, no child abuse, none of your city filth and corruption, your obscenities and perversion. We don't have it and we don't want it. So you'd better get yourselves out of town—and right on out of the county—or you're going to find yourselves in more trouble than you ever thought about in your whole, filthy life."

"Filthy life? Filthy life? Just who do you—" Dad had apparently forgotten the gun. Mom cleared her throat loudly, and he stopped. Even the back of Dad's neck was red. He ran his hand through his hair again and shuddered all over. "All right, sheriff, we will be gone as soon as—"

"You've got fifteen minutes. If you're not out of here in fifteen minutes, you are going to find yourself behind bars, mister. We have laws about your kind. I'd jail you this minute, except we don't want you and this—this obscenity"—he made a gesture that seemed to refer to *Brunhilda*—"in our town. Half an hour from now there could be children coming to this park, and you will not be here to corrupt their minds, you understand that?"

"Fifteen minutes," Dad repeated. "I wouldn't stay in Orville Corners for ten." He grabbed the inside handle, slammed the door in the sheriff's face, and locked it. "Rick," he said, "get down from there so we can put up your bunk. We're out of here. Now!"

Rick, his eyes as big and round as Ping-Pong balls, jumped down. "What did that man mean, Daddy? What's an obscenity?"

"Never mind. And I haven't the slightest idea what he means. He's probably insane. Or drunk. Or high on something."

"Isn't he a sheriff?"

"For all I know he could be a crazed homicidal maniac, but we're not hanging around to find out."

Mom was up and getting dressed. "Get your clothes on, kids," she said. "Jenny, get anything put away that can't be left out when we get moving."

We scrambled around and got dressed. I could practically

hear the seconds ticking off in my mind. I wondered what would happen if it took us more than fifteen minutes to get started. Would somebody start shooting? Would they really put Dad in jail?

"Does this mean we can't eat at EAT?" Rick asked.

"Not if we were starving to death!" Dad bellowed. He started the engine. Chatter started meowing, so I picked her up and threw her onto my bed and slammed the door.

Dad put *Brunhilda* in gear, and we moved away from the curb. He'd said ten minutes and it had taken us more like seven. The beds were still down; nobody'd had time to go to the bathroom or brush teeth or anything. All we wanted was to get out of there. Marcia opened the blinds over the swivel chairs and sat down. "Ugly town anyway," she said.

"The armpit of the state," Ben added.

Mom, seat-belted into her captain's chair, shook her head. "There must be something seriously wrong with that man."

"Inbreeding," Dad said. "Generations of inbreeding in a small town where the gene pool is limited. Causes brain damage."

Mom was looking out the window as we stopped for a red light at the bar and tabernacle intersection. "Michael, you may be right. Those men over there are staring at us and pointing. Do you suppose they've never seen a motor home before?"

"Nobody stared at us when we came through town yesterday," Marcia said.

"Those creeps on the village green last night stared," I said. It made me shiver to remember them. Bits of nightmare I couldn't quite remember flashed through my mind—like the taste that stays in your mouth when you bite into something rotten.

Rick was sitting on Mom and Dad's bed with Czar Nicholas in his lap. "Well, I wanted to have breakfast at EAT! Can't we just—"

"Don't be ridiculous," Dad said. "No force on the face of this earth could drag me back to Orville Corners for any reason whatsoever. Not if lives depended on it! Certainly not to eat at a place like that. Ptomaine poisoning. Botulism. That place probably contributes to the wholesale brain damage of the citizens of Orville Corners."

I looked out the window to see the welcome sign fall behind us. "Welcome to Orville Corners. Some welcome!"

"That madman's following us," Dad shouted. "I've half a mind—"

"Just keep going," Mom said. "Let's not have any more trouble."

"It's not just the people in Orville Corners," Marcia said.

"What?"

"We just passed a farm where an old man and an old woman were out hoeing in a garden, and they stared at us, too. And then the old woman shook her fist at us."

"At us? Marcia, you must be imagining—"

"No, Mom, she shook her fist right at us!"

Dad was looking in his side-view mirror. "The sheriff's still there, the lunatic. He's probably going to follow us clear to the county line."

"Who cares? The sooner we put this county behind us, the better I'll feel," Mom said. "People staring. Old women shaking their fists."

It was early enough that there wasn't a lot of traffic on

the road, but now a car came toward us. As it got close its horn started blaring and went right on till it was long past. "The driver of that car, too!" Dad said.

"What about him?"

"He shook his fist as he went by. And honked. Have we crossed over into the twilight zone, or what?"

"Nee nee noo nee, nee nee noo nee," Ben sang.

"I'm hungry!" Rick said. "I want some breakfast."

"We'll stop someplace," Dad said, "as soon as we leave this nest of nuts behind."

"Real people," Marcia whispered.

"Real people invented by Stephen King," I said. "Real sickos."

We drove for nearly half an hour after we'd passed the county line and the sheriff had stopped and turned back, before Dad would even consider looking for a place to eat. But, finally, he saw a truck stop and pulled into the parking lot. There was a semi parked there, its driver leaning against his window with his eyes closed. As we stopped, he looked up, grinned, and waved. Dad waved back. "Well, finally. A normal, friendly human being."

Mom undid her seat belt. "You kids go on inside and see what's on the breakfast menu. I'll take care of putting away the beds."

"I want waffles!" Rick said. "With blueberry syrup and sausage and grape juice . . ."

"Today, you can all have anything you want."

"Anything?" Ben asked.

"From the breakfast menu."

I was the first one out of the door, visions of bacon and hash browns and a giant stack of pancakes filling my mind. That's how I was the one who saw it first. Actually, I wouldn't have noticed except Rick, who'd pushed past Marcia in his hurry to get out, fell down the steps and let out a shriek that practically curdled my blood. I turned back to see what had happened, and that's when I saw. And understood. Everything.

Across *Brunhilda*'s side, in spray-painted letters about two feet high, were some words I can't repeat on this page. Next to the door under the front window were the words DOPE DEN. I just stood there, with my mouth hanging open. Rick didn't even bother to cry. He saw the expression on my face and turned around to see what I was looking at. Marcia did the same. Then Ben.

"Dad!" Ben called back inside. "You'd better come out here."

Something in Ben's tone of voice brought Mom and Dad out and down the stairs in a flash. Dad looked, then walked slowly all the way around. The rest of us followed him. There were more words on the front bumper and more on the other side. The worst of all were on the back.

"Well," Dad said, "I guess that explains that."

"Yeah," Marcia said. "And that truck driver's probably some disgusting pervert, grinning and waving like that."

"Rags!" Mom said. "Rags and paint thinner!"

"We don't have either," Dad pointed out.

"Well, then, Michael, we will have to get them. I don't intend to go another foot with words like that splattered all over us."

"I'll see if they have anything we can use at the truck stop."

"Aren't we going to eat first?" Rick asked. "I'm starving!"

"We are going to get those words scrubbed off—"

"What difference does it make?" Dad asked. "Let's eat

first and worry about the graffiti afterward. After all, we've already been labeled drug addicts and child abusers. How much worse can it get?"

Mom shook her head. "It wasn't so bad when we didn't know what the man was talking about. Now . . ."

"I'm starving!" This was Rick again. I didn't know which I wanted more—food or getting that paint off *Brunhilda*. It was embarrassing just standing next to her. Pancakes won, though. After all, we'd be inside the truck stop, and nobody had to know we belonged to the Dope Den.

"All right, we'll eat first," Mom said. "But I won't go another foot—"

"Right," Dad said. "Agreed."

And so we had a respite from catastrophe long enough to consume the biggest, most extravagant breakfast we'd had since we'd left home. Some people came in while we were eating and talked to the waitress about *Brunhilda;* another truck driver thought it was funny; but a middle-aged couple was badly upset. They said they'd have refused to stop at all if they hadn't been having breakfast here for twenty years. They were all for making the waitress refuse service to the "scum" from that bus. We must have looked too clean-cut and normal to belong to poor *Brunhilda,* because neither the couple nor the waitress so much as glanced our way.

We all took a very long time eating. I don't think any of us wanted to go back outside. But, finally, after Mom and Dad had had three cups of coffee each and Mom had refused to let Rick have dessert, we couldn't put it off any longer.

"You wouldn't happen to have any paint thinner, would you?" Dad asked, as he paid the bill. "And rags?"

"Paint thinner? Youse want paint thinner?"

And so Dad had to explain. When he'd finished, the woman was practically hysterical with laughter. "Them town kids!" she shrieked. "Them kids 'ud do anything for a laugh. Din't youse hear 'em doin' it?"

"If we'd heard them, we would have stopped them," Dad pointed out, his voice frosty.

She didn't seem to notice his tone. "Yeah. Sure." She collapsed into giggles again. "If youse knew Orville Corners, you'd a never stopped there in the first place."

"Paint thinner?" Dad asked again. "Rags?"

"Oh, sure, I can prob'ly find youse somethin'." She shook her head. "I'm real sorry for laughin', folks, but I can see 'em now, creepin' around in the middle a the night, shushin' each other so's they wouldn't wake youse up." She started to giggle again and then made an effort to stop. It didn't work. "Be right back," she said, and was still laughing when she disappeared into the kitchen.

"A sophisticated sense of humor," Dad said.

"Now who's being judgmental?" Mom said. "The fact is, if it hadn't been us it happened to, you'd be laughing as hard as she is."

Dad didn't answer. "Rick," he said, "go get Buffy and take her for a walk before she bursts."

"Ah, Dad, it's Ben's turn."

"You heard me, Rick."

The rest of us stayed inside when Rick went out. I, for one, wasn't going to be seen next to *Brunhilda* until I had to be.

In a matter of seconds Rick was back, tears brimming over in his eyes. "She's not there!" he said. "Buffy's not there!"

"What are you talking about? Of course . . ." Dad stopped. As if an electric shock had gone through us at the same time, we all remembered. I could see it clearly in my mind—Buffy pushing out past Dad when the door had opened that morning. We'd been in such a hurry to get out of Orville Corners, nobody had once thought to get Buffy back inside.

..... Rain, Rain, Rain .....

"We have to go back. Right this minute!" Rick wailed. "She'll be hit by a car! She'll be dog-napped."

"Some of those creeps'll probably poison her," Ben said. Rick howled.

"He didn't mean it," Mom said. "Nobody will poison her. And she's street smart. She won't get hit by a car."

"But she does go right up to people," Marcia said. "Anybody could pick her up."

"We'll never see Buffy again!" Rick was working toward genuine hysterics.

"Don't be silly. Of course we'll see her again." Mom's voice didn't sound as certain as her words. "We'll go back for her the minute we get that paint off."

"*Now, now, now!*" Rick screamed. "We have to go back for her now!"

"Eleanor," Dad said. "It'll take hours to get it all off."

"Well, we can't go back into Orville Corners this way! That wild man of a sheriff would probably open fire."

Just then the waitress came back. "Sorry, folks, youse'll have to go over to the hardware and paint store in Millville. I couldn't find anything that'd work." She held up some ragged pieces of cloth. "I found some rags, though."

"How far's Millville?" Dad asked.

"Not far. 'Bout five miles."

114

"And how will the residents of Millville feel about what's written on our vehicle?" Mom asked.

The waitress started laughing again. "Depends on which ones you run into. The chief of police over there's a Baptist."

Mom shook her head. "Michael, I am not budging out of this parking lot until we get rid of that paint."

Rick started wailing again. "Buffy'll be dead by that time. If she isn't already!"

While Mom and Dad had been having their third cup of coffee, I'd gone over to the jukebox to see what songs they had, and I'd noticed this big crack across the front of it— a crack that somebody had fixed with silver tape. The roll of tape was still sitting on top of the jukebox. Perfect!

"We could cover the paint with tape," I said.

The waitress said we could have the tape—no charge— and she even found another roll for us. So it took less than fifteen minutes to get *Brunhilda* presentable again. She looked a little weird, with these patches of silver tape all over, but nobody would call us filthy dope fiends anymore.

All the way back to Orville Corners Dad grumbled. Rick kept coming up with new horror stories about what could be happening to Buffy. Marcia sat at the dinette table with her hands folded and a crease in her forehead. Ben, as usual, was quiet. I, of course, visualized every one of Rick's catastrophes.

When we got to where we could just see the WELCOME TO ORVILLE CORNERS sign ahead, Dad pulled off onto the shoulder of the road and stopped.

"What's the matter?" Mom asked. "Why did you stop?"

"Because I am not taking *Brunhilda* into that town."

"But Buffy . . ." Rick howled.

"It is no more than a quarter of a mile from the town

limits to that green. She's probably right there where we left her. You kids can take her leash and walk in."

Mom started to protest, but Dad shushed her. "That sheriff didn't see the kids. Nobody will recognize them. And, anyway, they'll have a better chance of finding her on foot."

So we got the leash and started walking as fast as we could. "They've probably spray-painted *her* by now," Ben said. "Let's move."

Rick had to run to keep up. "Would paint kill her?"

"Don't be silly," Marcia said. "Nobody's going to paint her. Anyway, those guys wouldn't even know who she is or where she comes from. What worries me is how she feels. Betrayed, Abandoned."

That was what I was thinking about, too. What must she have thought when she came back and found *Brunhilda* gone? Deserted in a strange place by the only family she'd ever known. "What if she didn't stay there? What if she started off to try to find us?" I said.

"Yeah, like that story about the animals who walked thousands of miles." Marcia's eyes filled with tears.

I envisioned her setting out to go home to Pennsylvania. Where else would she go? She wouldn't know about the campground we'd decided to go to. I could see her, with cut and bleeding feet trudging along an interstate, trucks rushing past, her ribs showing through her once golden, now muddy and tangled, coat. She'd be on the edge of starvation. Alone, unloved, confused, and, most of all, betrayed. Trying to find her home and family. I blinked as the cracked sidewalk in front of me blurred. Another minute, and I'd be wailing like Rick.

"Dad's right," Ben said. "She's probably still at the village green, waiting for us." He was trying to sound brave, but he picked up the pace again, until we were all jogging. Rick had to quit crying because he didn't have the breath to cry and run at the same time. We passed the run-down houses, the dusty and depressing stores, the boarded-up windows, and finally The Rock Solid Christian Tabernacle. Finally I could see the Union soldier statue. The old men were back on their benches, and what looked like the same checkers game was going on. More people were there now, too. But it must have been too early for the teenage punks. They were probably all sleeping after their hard night of spray-painting. On their bench were two women with strollers.

"Buffy!" Rick shrieked. "Buffy!"

She was there, all right, sitting between the two strollers, looking up into the faces of the women and wagging her tail. She glanced toward us as she heard Rick's voice and then looked back at the women. One of them reached into a white paper bag that was sitting next to her on the bench and pulled out a doughnut. She broke it in two and handed one piece to her kid and the other to Buffy, who gulped it down and wagged her tail harder. Then she licked the kid's hand. By this time we were nearly there.

"Buffy!" Rick yelled again.

Buffy looked toward us again but didn't move. Apparently the white bag wasn't empty yet. But she never had a chance to get more doughnut, because Rick, with what must have been his last burst of energy, ran to her and flung his arms around her neck.

We clipped her leash to her collar, and after assuring the women that she was really ours, headed back to *Brunhilda*, a little more slowly.

"Buffy would take a doughnut over her own family," Ben grumped. "She didn't even miss us—probably didn't know we'd been gone."

"That's not true." Rick patted Buffy as we walked. "She trusts us, that's all. She knew we'd come back for her."

It was as good an explanation as any, I thought. At least she hadn't started back to Pennsylvania on her own.

By the time we got back to *Brunhilda* and listened to Mom and Dad make such a fuss over Buffy that it was clear they'd been just as scared as we were, I was wiped out. The day had started too early. When Dad got *Brunhilda* turned around and back on the road, I went to bed.

When I woke up, Chatter was rubbing my shoulder and meowing in my ear, and *Brunhilda* was stopped. There was a lot of extra noise I finally identified as rain beating on the roof and windows. Marcia opened the door. "You want lunch?"

"Is a pig pork? Of course I want lunch. What time is it?"

"Nearly one."

"Where are we?"

"At a roadside picnic ground."

We ate sandwiches and potato chips and sat, looking out at the soaked picnic area.

"This is what's so great about motor homes," Dad said. "We can have a picnic even in the rain."

"How far's the campground from here?" Ben asked.

"As slippery as these roads are, it'll probably take about two hours. We're really into mountains now, and *Brunhilda*'s not crazy about mountains."

"I don't much like driving in this rain," Mom said. "It makes me nervous."

Dad peered up at the sky. "Doesn't look as if it's going

to quit anytime soon. I'll drive carefully. And just think how nice it'll be to camp this way if it keeps raining tonight. No water coming through the tent, no need to dig trenches, no getting soaked on the way to the outhouse. The rain won't be any problem."

Like some other predictions Dad has made in his time, this did not turn out to be strictly true.

It's true that we didn't have to run through the rain to the bathroom. And it's true that the rain didn't leak in on us. Our beds and sleeping bags stayed dry. But there were six of us, and *Brunhilda* was only thirty-five feet long and eight feet wide. And it kept raining. And raining.

To be fair, the first day wasn't all that bad. Everybody was tired, and it seemed kind of fun just to hang out and read and listen to the television—here we got bearable sound on two channels, even though there was no picture— while the rain drummed on overhead. Mom had packed ponchos for everybody, so we explored the campground a little and only our sneakers and socks got wet. It wasn't even so awful taking Buffy out at first. I wrote letters to Jason and Sarah and listened to my Walkman, and Marcia worked on her wild edible food report; Mom wrote a column about camping in the rain; Rick played with his G.I. Joe figures, and Ben read *My Side of the Mountain* for what must have been the thirtieth time. After Orville Corners Dad lost interest in reading *Blue Highways* for some reason and bought a spy thriller at the campground store. So that first day was all right.

But it was still raining the next morning. It was still raining at lunchtime. Mom organized a rain hike that Dad refused to join, and on which both Rick and Marcia slipped off the trail and ended up covered in mud. We ran out of

groceries and had to walk to the store for more. On the way
back, two of the bag bottoms disintegrated—one of them
the one that had the eggs. Dad found a regional newspaper
that listed a movie he wanted to see in a nearby town, but
then we realized that the only way to go to the movie was
to drive *Brunhilda*, whose wheels were sunk into the mud
so far Dad wasn't sure he'd ever get out.

That was the night Buffy put her muddy paws all over
Dad's last clean shirt when she came in from her walk. At
least the next morning there was something to do. We took
the laundry to the campground's Laundromat. By the time
we got it back the clothes were all wet again, and we had
to drape things all over the furniture to dry.

As I said before, the cats hadn't been any trouble on this
trip, except for Chatter's noise whenever *Brunhilda* was
moving. Both cats were indoor cats anyway, they slept a
lot, and unlike Buffy they didn't take up floor space when
they slept. But now, in the rain, this changed. Chatter went
out when we were bringing the laundry back. Mom said
she'd be back in no time because she'd hate the rain. But
she didn't come right back. She was gone for hours, and
when she did come back, she was soaked. But she didn't
seem to mind. She came in churring and trilling, rubbed
her wet fur all along the front of the couch, leaving muddy
paw prints behind her, jumped up on the dinette, and
dropped a present right in the middle of the table, where
Rick had set up a G.I. Joe base. What she dropped, mere
inches from the nose of Rick, the world's most passionate
rodent lover, was a wet, muddy, bloody, decapitated mouse.

Rick didn't recover the rest of that evening. He cried
himself to sleep. By that time the Skinner family's nerves

were in tatters. What we all needed was sunshine. Swimming. Hiking. Space. Most of all, space.

What we got, as everybody discovered the moment we opened our eyes the next morning, was more rain. By ten A.M. Mom had set all four of us kids to playing Monopoly. She and Dad sat in the living room playing cribbage. Buffy, evicted from under their feet, came to lie under ours and was shooed back to them. Dad put her in Marcia's and my bedroom, where she howled. Ben opened the door for her, and she went back under Mom's and Dad's feet. They shooed her to us. We shooed her to them. Finally, breaking every rule Buffy's ever been given about furniture, Dad lifted her bodily onto the couch, where she spent the rest of the morning curled, guiltily pretending to be asleep.

"You took eight steps, not seven!" Ben said, as Marcia missed landing on Vermont Avenue, where he had two hotels.

"I took seven," Marcia said.

"Eight!"

"Seven!"

"Do I have to come over there?" Dad asked.

I threw the dice. And landed on the Short Line Railroad. "Anybody own it?"

"I do," Rick said. "Pay me."

"You own Pennsylvania, not Short Line."

"Short Line!"

"Look for yourself," I said. "You don't have the Short Line card."

"Somebody stole it!" Rick shrieked.

"You never had it!" Ben said.

"Did too!"

"Did not." This was Marcia.

"Cheaters, cheaters, cheaters," Rick yelled.

"Rick Skinner, you're outnumbered," Mom said. "That's enough."

"Cheaters," he repeated, but more quietly.

"Well, are you going to buy it?" Marcia asked. Marcia, as usual, was banker.

It occurred to me that I hated Monopoly. Always had, always would. "No. Your turn, Rick."

"Cheaters," Rick said, and rolled doubles. He landed on Go to Jail and didn't roll doubles the second time, so he couldn't get out. He burst into tears.

Dad threw his cards on the table and came over to our game. "That's enough. If you can't play without all this squabbling and carping, you're not to play at all. I've never heard anything so childish in my life." He folded up the board so that all the pieces and houses, hotels and cards fell into the center. He dumped them into the box lid.

"Hey, I was winning!" Ben protested.

"You were not. I was." This was Marcia.

"Enough! Go to your rooms."

We just looked at him.

"Oh," he said. "Well—put on your ponchos and go outside."

"It's lunchtime," Rick said.

"Fine. Put this game away and we'll have lunch."

"Then what?" Ben asked.

"Maybe it will have stopped raining by then," Mom said.

"Ellie, there is optimism, and then there is an inability to stay in touch with reality."

"Oh, hush. It's your turn to fix lunch."

Chatter got out again when Mom took Buffy for her midday walk. Once a cat quits being an indoor cat, it's impossible to keep it inside. She had hidden under the swivel chair and streaked past the minute Mom opened the door. It sounded to me as if Dad muttered "good riddance" under his breath, but I couldn't be sure.

"After lunch," Dad announced while we ate, "we will play an adult game, with adult supervision. No more accusations of cheating, no more arguments. We'll play team Trivial Pursuit—your mother heading one team, myself heading the other."

"I want to be on Mom's team," Rick said.

"Teams will be chosen by lot," Dad replied. "There is to be no possibility of argument and unpleasantness."

Rick and Marcia were on Mom's team, Ben and me on Dad's. Marcia was put in charge of the question cards.

For half an hour or so things went fine. Team leaders were allowed to pick which way they'd move around the board once they'd rolled the dice, so there wouldn't be any arguments about what kind of question the team would have to answer, and that worked. Teams were allowed to talk the answers over so that they wouldn't miss a question if one member happened to shout out the wrong answer. That worked, too.

And then, on our team's turn, things began to go sour.

" 'What's fiddler's green?' " Marcia read.

"Repeat the question, please," Dad said.

"What's fiddler's green?"

"No, Marcia, our category is Science."

"That's the Science question. What's fiddler's green?"

"That's nothing to do with science," Dad said.

"Never mind," Mom said. "Just answer it."

"It's the principle of the thing, Ellie. We should have a

Science question. Fiddler's green is not a Science question."

"The game calls it a Science question."

"The game's wrong!"

"Nobody said it was perfect, Michael. Answer the question."

Dad looked at Ben, then at me. "Well?"

I shrugged. "Never heard of it."

"Me neither," Ben said.

"Do you know the answer or not?" Mom said.

Dad frowned. "Just a minute, just a minute. Fiddler's green. Fiddler's green." There was a long silence. Finally, he looked at Marcia. "I don't know. What is it?"

" 'Sailors' heaven,' " Marcia read.

"What?"

"Sailors' heaven."

"That's ridiculous!"

"Well, what is it, then?" Marcia asked. "That's what it says on the card."

"I don't know what it is," Dad yelled, "but sailors' heaven? What's that got to do with Science?"

"It's Science and Nature," Marcia said.

"What's sailors' heaven got to do with Nature?"

"You missed. It's our turn," Rick said.

Mom rolled the dice. Dad fidgeted and sighed all the way through their turn. When they answered a History question correctly and got their yellow wedge, Dad sighed louder than ever. But he rolled the dice.

We didn't get that question right either. On Mom's team's next turn, they landed on a Sports question.

" 'What game room is on a Clue board?' " Marcia read.

"A billiard room!" Rick yelled.

Marcia turned the card over. "Right."

"That was supposed to be a Sports question," Dad said. "What does a stupid board game have to do with sports?"

"It's Sports and Leisure Activities," Mom pointed out.

"But Clue? Come on. Our last Sports question was really hard. To say nothing of the fiddler's green travesty."

It was Mom's turn to sigh. "The degree of difficulty varies," she said. "Sometimes we get an easy one, sometimes you get an easy one."

"Just because I knew the answer doesn't mean it was easy," Rick protested.

"It was easy," Dad said.

"Did *you* know it?"

"It was easy, Rick." Two questions later Dad took Ben's answer for a History question, and when we were wrong, he threatened to throw him off the team. Ben pointed out that Dad's answer wasn't right either.

Then there was a small lull. Dad got two answers right while Mom and her team missed five in a row. "Good game, this," Dad said. He was smiling steadily.

Mom was very strong. She didn't mention fiddler's green.

An hour later, we were neck and neck. Both teams had gotten all their wedges, and whoever got to the center first and answered a final question would be the winner. It was our turn. Dad rolled a five. We were only three moves from the center, so we had to go through and up the other side.

Mom rolled a four and was within one space of the center.

Dad rolled another four and had to go through the center again and up the other side.

Mom rolled a six.

Dad rolled a five.

Mom rolled a five and landed in the center.

"No fair!" Dad said. "We got all our wedges before you did. That roll of the dice was pure luck."

"It's how the game is played," Mom said.

"Well, it's ridiculous!"

"What category do you choose for us?" Marcia asked.

"Sports," Ben said. "They're worst at Sports."

"Don't forget Clue," Dad said. "Give them History."

"Sports," Ben said.

"History."

"Sports."

"How about Arts and Literature," I suggested, hoping to break the deadlock. I didn't care. I just wanted to be done with the game.

"Are you crazy?" Dad asked. "Your mother's terrific at Arts and Literature!"

"Geography, then," Ben said. "None of us can do Geography worth anything."

"Okay. Geography."

Marcia picked the next card. " 'What city is served by Dulles International Airport?' "

"Cheat!" Dad shouted. "Cheat!"

"What do you mean, cheat?" Mom asked. Her voice was like dry ice.

"That's the easiest question we've had this whole game. One of our Geography questions was about Ulan Bator. Who in the world has ever heard of Ulan Bator?"

"The people of Mongolia," Marcia said.

"May we answer our question now?" Mom asked, her voice still freezing. "You did choose the category."

"I told you we should have chosen History," Dad said to Ben.

"Washington, D.C.," Mom said.

"Right," Marcia said. "We won."

"Hurray!" Rick said. "We won, we won, we won!"

Dad dropped our game piece into the box and stood up. "Stupidest game I've ever played."

Mom smiled a frosty smile. "An adult game," she said. "I believe that's what you called it."

"Come on, Buffy, it's time for your walk." Dad put Buffy's leash on her and took her out into the rain.

"Your poncho!" Rick called after him. Dad didn't answer.

Just before the door slammed, Chatter scooted in, wet, muddy, and churring. She leaped to the middle of the game board and proudly dropped two-thirds of a chipmunk.

...... Outward Bound ......

It was still dark when I opened my eyes. There was no light inside *Brunhilda* and no light outside. It took me a moment to figure out what had wakened me. Not a dream. Not a cat walking on me. Maybe a noise? Then I knew. It was quiet. Very, very quiet. There was no sound of rain on the roof. I peered out between the slats of the blinds next to me. There was a little light—maybe starlight, maybe moonlight—so I could make out the motor home next to us, a gray presence. Starlight or moonlight, it must mean the clouds were gone.

Instead of a day of probable madness and possible homicide, we could look forward to a day in which we could be as far from each other as we wanted to be. I doubted if there would be two Skinners within a mile of each other from breakfast on. And I knew what my day would be like. I'd head for this park's beach. It would be wonderful. No Mom and Dad snapping at each other. No irritating Rick with his little plastic men and his war noises. No sullen, silent Ben. No Marcia with her interminable lectures on subjects nobody else cared about. Sun, water, solitude. And guys.

I went to sleep again with these happy visions moving through my brain. But it didn't take very long, once morning came, to dispel them.

128

"Your father and I went out early this morning for a long walk, and we've had a wonderful idea!" Mom said, pouring pancake batter onto the griddle. Brilliant sunshine streamed through the galley window.

Ben had just finished turning his bed back into a dinette. "You went for a walk?" he asked. "Together?"

"After that game, I thought you weren't speaking to each other," Marcia observed as she set the living-room table.

"Of course we're speaking to each other," Mom said. "We're adults, after all. And it was only a game."

Dad came out of the bathroom and squeezed past Mom. It looked to me as if he patted her on the behind on the way. "Only a game. Besides, today's a new day. A beautiful day. The sun is shining, the birds are singing, and all's right with the world."

This was a possible exaggeration, but after all that rain, it was forgivable.

"So what's the idea?" Ben asked. He sounded suspicious. It was true that both Mom and Dad seemed almost unnaturally cheerful, even considering the sunshine.

"Have you ever heard of Outward Bound?" Mom asked.

"Isn't that a place where business executives take wilderness survival training?" Marcia asked.

"Sort of. Not only business executives—anybody. The real program is in several places, but I just mean the idea. Other groups call it other things."

"What is the idea?" Ben asked.

"To teach people some things about themselves, and how to cooperate with and rely on others."

Dad grinned this enormous grin. It reminded me of the way he looked when he first started talking about At Your Service. It was not an expression we had learned to trust.

"Your mother and I thought the four of you could use a little of that Outward Bound experience. We noticed a certain—a certain lack of brotherly and sisterly love and cooperation over the last few days. So we've decided to sponsor a Skinner Offspring Outward Bound Experience."

Just then Rick, who'd been out walking Buffy, opened the door. "Do I have to tie Buffy outside?" he asked. "The ground's still wet."

Dad's cheerfulness slipped for one moment. "Keep that dog and her muddy paws out of here!"

"Okay, but . . ."

"Close the door!" Mom shouted, but she was too late. Chatter scooted out between Rick's legs. I wondered what it would be this time. If her kills kept getting bigger, she'd bring in a bear's hindquarter soon. Rick, who was having trouble reconciling his love for Chatter and her passion for murder and dismemberment, went off to chase her down. Later, he complained that if he'd been there when the Outward Bound Experience was fully explained, he wouldn't have agreed to it. Much good that would have done. Skinner offspring never have to agree to anything in order for it to happen. This was no exception.

While we took turns eating the stacks of pancakes Mom was turning out, Dad explained what was going to happen. Since Ben had proven his ability to survive in the wild, he would be designated leader of the Experience. We were all to cooperate and offer our own suggestions and ideas, but Ben was to be the final decision maker. I groaned at this part. I looked across the table at him, where he was mopping up syrup with the last bite of pancake, expecting him to be visibly swelling with importance, and was surprised to see his expression. He didn't look as if he liked the idea at all.

The plan was that we would be provided with a few basic necessities and abandoned (That isn't the word Mom and Dad used, of course) in a designated wilderness area. We would hike until we found a good site for setting up camp. We were to return to *Brunhilda* at noon the next day.

"You will have to depend on each other," Mom said. "Share and cooperate."

All my joyous visions of freedom from my family crumbled to dust.

Dad put his arm around Mom and she leaned against him. After last night, they were curiously together on this. And curiously happy about it.

"What basic necessities do we get to take?" Marcia asked, with her usual good sense. This was clearly something we needed to know.

"Sleeping bags, backpacking tents, canteens of fresh water . . ." Mom started.

"Matches," Ben said.

"Of course, matches. Flashlights, compass, cooking utensils . . ."

"What food?" This was from me.

Mom grinned. "With the fisherman and the edible wild plants expert along, you won't need to take food."

I looked at Marcia and she looked at me. Even Marcia didn't like the idea of living on fish and leaves! "No food!"

"All right, you can take some dried soup as a backup. And some jerky."

Jerky. As far as I was concerned, we might as well take Buffy's rawhide bones.

"Do we have to do this?" Ben asked. I was surprised. This was the kind of thing Ben should have jumped at. He was the one who'd been so hot to get into the Adirondacks and what he called "real wilderness." Maybe he just didn't want to have the rest of us along. That was fine with me. I didn't want to have any part of it.

Neither Mom nor Dad answered this directly. I think they wanted to preserve the idea that this was a family decision.

"That's why we're having pancakes this morning," Mom said. "So you'll be starting off well fortified."

"When is this supposed to start?" Marcia asked.

"Right after breakfast," Dad said.

Rick returned in tears. He'd failed to catch Chatter, so he considered himself an accomplice in whatever murder she committed this time. Mom gave him pancakes to cheer him up, but the outline he got of the Outward Bound Experience was sketchy at best. He seemed to be the only one of us who thought it sounded like fun. We realized later this was because nobody had explained to him about the food.

We spent an hour or so getting ready. Ben and I were to wear the big frame packs carrying all four sleeping bags, the two two-person tents, and the extra clothes; Marcia and Rick were to wear regular backpacks with the food, water, flashlights, cooking stuff, etc.

On their early walk Mom and Dad had picked up a trail map of the area where we were being abandoned. This they gave to Ben. Mom and Dad were to walk with us to the beginning of the trail. As we walked, I felt like Hansel and Gretel. But Mom and Dad were positively glowing with enthusiasm.

"You'll have the most wonderful time!" Mom said.

"You could go with us," Rick said. "We'd let you."

"No, no. This is for you kids. You'll come back feeling so good—so self-confident, so pleased with yourself and each other." Mom looked at Ben, who was sort of hunched forward under his backpack, looking at the ground as he walked. "You know how that is, don't you, Ben? You've done it. You've already had that experience."

"Mmm," Ben said. He didn't sound very self-confident or pleased with himself to me.

Finally, we came to the sign that marked the beginning of the trail. It was named for a mountain. I wondered how big the mountain was. Ominously, the sign claimed the trail to be a ten-mile loop. Already the straps of the backpack were digging into my shoulders. If I had to walk ten miles I would almost certainly die. "You're sure there aren't bears," I said.

"There aren't bears."

"What about slashers?"

"There are four of you," Dad said.

"Yeah, four kids against a machete!"

"There aren't slashers," Mom said.

"Watch for Chatter," Rick said. "And don't let her out again!"

"We'll try, but we can't promise anything. She's too quick."

"Bury whatever she brings home." In spite of the rain, Rick had had two solemn funerals for the mouse and the chipmunk part. "And don't forget the cross."

"Right." Dad put his arm around Mom and grinned at us. "You'll be close enough that one of you could come back for help if you need to. But I'm sure you won't need to. Ben's an expert, after all, and you're all bright and resourceful. Have a great time!"

Then they each kissed us all good-bye. I was reminded
of that movie about the sinking of the *Titanic,* when the
women and children were getting into the lifeboats. Only
in this case, Mom and Dad were in the lifeboat, and we
were being put onto the *Titanic.*

"Okay, Ben," Mom said, "lead your forces. We'll see you
tomorrow for lunch."

Ben mumbled something and started up the trail. He was
not sounding like a great leader. But there was nothing for
the rest of us to do but follow him. After all, I told myself,
we weren't going to be that far from Mom and Dad. We
were in a state park. We weren't setting off into the Amazon
Jungle.

Half an hour later, I thought the Amazon Jungle would
have been better. There, at least, you could float along
in a dugout canoe on the river. Here we had only our feet
and a trail that went up and up and up. Three times I told
Ben we should stop and set up camp, and three times he
said we couldn't put the tents up until we found some
flat ground. There wasn't so much as a square foot of flat
ground as far as the eye could see, which wasn't far, what
with the trees and undergrowth and rocks.

Worse, the trail was muddy and slippery. I kept turning
my ankle. My backpack began to weigh a hundred and fifty
pounds. And even though I'd had two stacks of pancakes,
I was starving. Maybe it was just the thought that we didn't
have any real food with us. I kept having visions of pizza,
melted cheese dripping off the edges, pepperoni and mushrooms stacked a quarter-inch deep.

Rick kept lagging behind, and we had to stop and wait
for him to catch up. It wasn't that I minded stopping—

anything to give my feet a rest—only that the longer it took us to get over this mountain, the longer it would be before we found flat ground and could stop for good. Once, while we were waiting, I made the mistake of sitting down on a rotten log. I might as well have sat down in a puddle. My bottom was soaked.

"Rotten logs are the forest's sponges," Marcia said. "They soak up tons of water when it rains, and when the ground dries out, they act like a kind of irrigation system and keep everything around them damp."

"Well, you might have warned me, Miss Know-It-All. I'm sopped. Anyway, this ground isn't going to dry out for weeks."

"Shut up," Ben said.

"Yes, sir!" I shouted, and snapped him a salute. "Anything you say, sir!"

"Can you see Rick yet?"

"No, but I can hear him. I think he's just on the other side of that bend in the trail down there."

"Let's go, then." Ben set off again.

Finally, we made it to the top of the mountain. But if I thought we could make camp on top, I soon gave up on the idea. It was nothing but rocks.

Rick appeared from among the tall shrubs lining the trail. His face was red, and his hair was plastered to his face with sweat. "Can we be done now?" he asked. "I'm tired."

Ben shook his head. "We can't camp up here. For one thing, there's no place to set up the tents. For another, this is a lousy place to find food." He was looking at the map. "We have to go on down the other side. At the bottom of the mountain there's a stream. Or a river. Anyway, there will be fish we can have for dinner."

"What are we going to catch them with?" Marcia asked.

"I brought fishing lines and hooks."

"What about bait?"

"As wet as the ground is, we won't have any trouble finding worms."

"What about lunch?" Rick asked. "I'm hungry. I want lunch."

"It's not time yet," Marcia said. "We've only been gone a little over an hour."

"I can't help it. I'm hungry!"

"Me, too," I said. "I don't know why, but I'm starved."

Marcia nodded. "Okay. Me, too."

"All we've got is that dried soup and the jerky," Ben said. "And to make the soup, we have to have a fire. I'd rather wait till we set up camp."

"I've got some granola bars," Marcia said, and shrugged off her backpack. "I sort of sneaked them in when Mom wasn't looking."

The good thing about the top of the mountain was that the sun was shining directly on it and the rocks were dry. We took off our backpacks, found places to sit down, and ate jerky and granola bars and drank water. In a little while, things began to look better. The view was spectacular, out over the mountains. Among the mountains sparkled lakes and streams. The sky was a deep, deep blue, and two hawks were circling high above us. "It's gorgeous up here," I said.

"Yeah." Marcia nodded. "I wonder how many miles we can see from up here."

"We'd better get going," Ben said. "The sooner we get down, the sooner we'll find a place to camp."

"At least going down will be easier," I said.

That shows you how much I knew about it. Going down

isn't easier at all. It's harder. My backpack kept wanting to go first—over my head. And my toes kept jamming up into the front of my hiking boots. The muddy trail made everything ten times worse. I slipped and fell so often I was tempted just to sit in the mud and slide down—except there were too many rocks. Not one of us made it to the bottom without falling, not even Ben.

Once we'd made it down, Ben stopped. I nearly ran into him.

"What's the matter?"

"I can't tell which is the trail. Can you?"

Now that we were at the bottom, trees towered over us and the sunlight could barely reach the ground. I couldn't see where the trail went either. There were three possibilities—to the right, to the left, and sort of straight ahead.

"Aren't there trail markers?"

"Do you see any?"

"Nope."

When Marcia and Rick arrived, they couldn't tell either. There weren't even any footprints to give us a clue. We must have been the first people to use the trail since the rain.

"You wait here, and I'll scout on up ahead to see which it is," Ben said. He took off his pack and headed off to the right.

"You want me to try another one?" I called.

"No. Just stay there."

After a while he came back and tried the left-hand possibility. Finally he tried the one in the middle.

"So?"

He shook his head. "Well, it isn't the one on the right. There's a huge tree down across that one."

"What does the map say?" Marcia asked.

"That we're at the corner of Elm and Main streets," Ben said.

"You don't have to be sarcastic."

"Look for yourself." Ben handed her the map, and she studied it for a while.

"I think it's the left one," Ben said. "The river's to the left here, and the trail finally goes along right next to it."

So we followed the trail to the left. Ben's idea was that as soon as we reached the river, we'd set up camp. I hoped we'd reach it soon. I was starving again.

For a while the trail was just the way it had been—muddy. But now, besides rocks to twist your ankle against, there were tree roots everywhere. I had to watch the ground every step of the way. Hiking is supposed to be a good way to enjoy the beauty of nature. You don't find the beauty of nature peering down at your feet and mud and rocks and roots.

But then things got even worse. Ben stepped off a rock onto what looked like moss and sank up to his ankles in black, oozy stuff. "Be careful," he called over his shoulder. He was too late. Just as I heard the words, I went in, too—right over the top of my hiking boots. Cold water ran down inside. Marcia, coming behind me, stopped in time, but Rick, who wasn't paying attention, bumped into her and knocked her in, too.

Ben tried going on ahead, but no matter which way he stepped, he was still in the ooze. Finally, he stepped up onto a tree root. Then, balancing carefully against the weight of his backpack, he stepped onto another. "You can do it if you stay up on the tree roots," he said.

Marcia pulled one foot out with a disgusting, sucking sound. "I don't think this is the trail," she said.

"Brilliant observation," Ben said.

"I'm tired," Rick said. "Let's camp here. I don't want to go into that stuff."

"We can't camp here," Ben said. "There's no solid ground."

"Let's go back, then."

"We are going to camp by the river."

"But this isn't the trail to the river," I reminded him.

"What does this look like, a desert? The river's got to be here somewhere."

And so we kept on through the swamp. Or bog. Bogs always sounded romantic to me. They aren't. Besides being cold in your boots, they smell bad.

Once Marcia stepped from one tree root to another, and the moment she got all her weight on it, it broke. She went sideways into the ooze from her toes to her neck, and I had to step in, too, to pull her up. From then on, of course, Marcia smelled like bog.

But there was something worse than the smell. Something worse even than the ooze itself. Bugs. Mosquitoes and flies of some kind that bit. Hard. We'd brought insect repellent, luckily, and we stopped and smeared it all over ourselves—even in our hair. But still the bugs stayed around us. Marcia said that deer had been driven crazy by flies and had run off cliffs or into rivers to get away. I could believe it.

As we went on, after that, I thought about the Tolkien books. It helped. I pretended I was in Mirkwood, on an adventure so vital that the future of Middle Earth, of the whole world, depended on it. No matter how rough the going might be, we had to go on.

Eventually, Ben turned out to be right. Eventually, we came to the river. And then we got out of the bog and onto ground that was merely muddy. And best of all, it was flat.

We set up camp at last, hanging our backpacks from tree limbs to keep them out of the mud and spreading plastic groundsheets to keep our sleeping bags dry. Then we all took off our wet boots and socks and went barefoot, which was much more comfortable. We washed out our muddy socks in the river and spread them on bushes to dry in the sun.

"Now, all you have to do is gather firewood," Ben said, "and start a fire. I'll catch some fish."

"And I'll pick some plants," Marcia said.

"I don't like plants," Rick complained, "or fish."

"Maybe we could catch a rabbit, then," Ben suggested. "I know how to make a trap."

"Eat a rabbit? Are you crazy?"

"So I'll catch fish."

"I'll eat granola bars," Rick said.

But when Marcia had fallen into the bog, the granola bars, which were in the outside pouch of her backpack, had gotten soaked. So had the envelopes of soup. We still had a few sticks of jerky.

I crawled into the tent I was to share with Marcia, and it wasn't bad. Almost cozy. It isn't easy to change clothes in one of those tents, but I was able to get my muddy jeans off and my extra pair on. When I came out, I looked around at our little campsite. Marcia had made a circle of rocks where we'd build our fire. Ben had made a sort of kitchen area on a flat rock, where he'd put the canteens and the cook set. It looked like a real campsite. And we'd done it all by ourselves! Marcia changed into her extra pair of jeans, then put on dry socks and got back into her hiking boots.

"Yuck, aren't those still wet?"

"Yes, but I'm not going to pick plants barefoot."

"She's right," Ben said. "Poison ivy. You two had better get your boots back on, too, so you can gather firewood."

Marcia went off on her own, Ben got out his fishing line and hooks, and Rick and I set off to find firewood. The sound of the river gurgling behind us was pleasant; the sun was warm on our shoulders; birds were calling to each other among the trees. Things were looking up. Camping was fun. Being on our own was fun. All we had to do now was to get some firewood, make a fire, and cook our food.

I took Rick's hand and started singing, " 'I love to go a-wandering, along a mountain track.' " He joined me. " 'And as I go, I love to sing, my knapsack on my back. Val-der-ee, val-der-ah, val-der-ee, val-der-ah-ha-ha-ha-ha-ha, val-der-ee . . .' "

.......Alone Together.......

If you stop to think for a moment, you will realize what happens when it rains in the woods for days and days. Things get wet. Not just trees and bushes and toadstools and rocks, but also sticks and branches, otherwise known as firewood. Every single stick Rick or I picked up was wet. Even the ones that were lying in the sun and looked dry were only dry on the top. Underneath they were just as wet as all the rest. We took a bunch of half-dry ones back to camp. It was the best we could do.

On the way back I gave Rick a mock nature lesson. "Here, Rick," I said, "you see a ground-hugging Budweiser vine with its distinctive red, white, and blue fruit."

"Is that anything like the Genesee vine?"

"A close relative. Note the similarity of the fruits. Too bad we can't burn beer cans."

"How about this? What plant is this from?" He held up a Coke bottle.

"Oh, Rick, let's take that back to camp. We can use it as a vase for wildflowers."

So when we got back to camp, we had with us eight medium-wet sticks and one Coke bottle. Ben was sitting on a rock, looking grumpy. "What're you doing back so soon?" I asked. "You catch our dinner already?"

142

He shook his head. "I haven't caught anything."

"Why not? Couldn't you find bait?"

"Oh, I found plenty of bait."

"So what's the problem?"

"No fish."

"No fish in the whole river?" Rick asked.

"No fish I can reach. There's a pool near the opposite bank that looks really neat—I'm just sure there are fish in it—but I can't reach it. I tried throwing the line every way I know how—even tied it on the end of a stick to use like a pole. But without a reel, I can't cast. The hook just goes out a little way and plops into the water."

"What did you do when you were out on your own before?"

Ben shifted on the rock. "That was a different stream."

Rick shrugged. "I don't like fish anyway."

"So where's the firewood?" Ben asked.

I held up the sticks. "This is it. Period. Everything out there's soaked. These aren't exactly dry."

"Where'd you get them?"

"These were in the sun, which is why at least one side's sort of dry."

"You were looking on the ground?"

"Of course! What'd you think we were doing, climbing trees?"

"Jenny, don't you know anything? You can't pick up firewood off the ground, especially when it's been raining."

"That's what I've been telling you."

"I mean, you look for the dead lower branches that are still on the trees. They dry out pretty fast after a rain and all you have to do is break them off. If they're really big, you can get them with a hatchet."

"Is that what you did?"

"Of course it is. Sometimes you find dead trees that are still standing, and if they're small enough, you can cut them down."

"Isn't cutting trees illegal?"

"Not if they're dead."

I shrugged. "Okay. Give me the hatchet and we'll go back again. Come on, Rick." I looked around. Rick wasn't anywhere to be seen. "Rick!" I called. "Come on! Where are you?"

There was a rustling in the bushes off to my right. "I'm over here. Just a minute."

I figured he had gone to find himself a wilderness rest room. "Hurry up, we have to go look for more wood."

His voice sounded strangely muffled. "Okay, just a minute."

While I was waiting, I went down to the water to fill the Coke bottle. I'd seen some yellow daisy things with dark centers that would look very pretty on our table rock—if we ever had anything to eat on it. I rinsed the bottle a couple of times. Then, as I was filling it again, I noticed the shape. It had a fairly long neck and that indentation—sort of hour-glassy, except not so skinny in the middle. I had an idea.

"Ben, come here!"

"What for?"

"Just come here. And bring your fishing stuff."

He came, but not very enthusiastically. "There's no good places there, Jenny. I've already tried right where you're standing. The water's not deep enough."

"No, no. Look here a minute." I poured the water out of the bottle. "Here's your reel."

"What are you talking about?"

"Give me the fishing line." I tied the line around the bottle at the narrow part. It couldn't slip either up toward the neck or down. Then I wound the line around and around and around, until about a yard from the end where the sinker and the hook (with its worm) were. "Now, watch. If this does what I think it'll do, you've got a casting rod." I held the bottle by the neck, swung the hook end of the line around and around my head, and let go. The line reeled off the bottle, and the hook and sinker splashed down way out in the deep water.

"Fantastic!" Ben said. He grabbed the bottle out of my hand. "Look, you can reel it in, too." He held the bottle sideways and turned it around and around, so the line wrapped itself back around the bottle. He jerked his head at me. "Go get the firewood, Jenny. We'll have a fish for dinner in no time."

So much for gratitude, I thought. "Come on, Rick! Let's get going."

Rick emerged from the bushes. His backpack was slung over one shoulder. "What's that for?" I asked.

He shrugged. "Uh, oh, well—don't we need something to carry the wood in?"

"How about our arms? It wouldn't fit in there anyway." I reached for his pack. "Let me hang it back up for you."

"No, that's okay. I'll do it."

You can never tell when kids are going to get funny about doing things themselves. I just grabbed the hatchet. The main thing we had to do was get that wood, or we'd never eat.

Half an hour later, Rick and I had a decent pile of firewood stacked next to the fire circle, and Ben had actually caught a fish. He came hollering up from the river with this fish dangling from the end of the line.

"Look, you guys! Dinner. I did it! I caught our dinner."

"Not mine," Rick said.

Ben ignored this. "I actually caught our dinner!"

"Good, but is that going to be enough? There are four of us—well, three, since Rick won't eat any."

"I'll get some more. But, Jenny, aren't you excited? I did it! I actually did it."

"That's great, Ben, but what's the big deal? You did that when you were out on your own before."

"Oh. Right. Well." Ben crouched near our rock table and took the hook out of the fish's mouth. "This is different. This is for all of us."

"Listen, before you go catch some more fish, how about getting the fire started? I'm not very good at this."

Ben dumped the fish into a pan and came over to build the fire. "You got the matches?"

I held them up. "Sure, but what do you light? At home we always use newspaper."

Ben laughed. "Campers don't use newspaper. They use tinder."

"What's tinder?" Rick asked.

"Dry grass, dry leaves . . ."

"Forget that," I said. "Forget dry anything!"

"Okay, so birch bark. Rick! Go find us some birch bark!"

Rick had vanished again, but he hadn't gone so far that he couldn't hear us. "Dad said we weren't allowed to peel birch bark," he shouted from the bushes where he'd been before.

"Not whole sheets. Just some little bits. It won't hurt a

birch tree to lose a few little shreds of bark."

"I'll get it," I said. "Anything else?"

"Get some of those little bitty dead twigs off a pine tree. There's resin in those, and they light real fast."

By the time I got back, Ben had a sort of tepee built out of the smaller sticks. He put the birch bark in the middle, crumpled up the pine twigs, and set them on top. Then he lit a match, which immediately blew out. I held my hands around the matchbox while he lit the next, and this one stayed lit. Shielding the flame, he carefully held it to a bit of birch bark. It crinkled a little and a blue line of flame appeared, which almost immediately caught the cluster of pine twigs above it. In no time, we had a tidy little fire started.

"I did it!" Ben shouted. "Come look, Rick, I did it. I started the fire!"

He was almost as excited as he'd been with the fish. "Big deal," I said.

"Oh, sure," he said. "Right. Big deal. Anybody can get a fire started with matches."

"Well, can't they?"

"If they know how."

Rick had appeared again. Again, he had his backpack. He hung it on the branch and came over to look at the fire. Just then, Marcia came out of the bushes, her arms full of plants. "A fire!" she said. "Hurray! I've got dinner."

"Part of dinner," Ben said. "I caught a fish!"

"Great. Meat and vegetables. Just like home."

"Yuck." This from Rick.

Marcia dumped her plants down on the ground next to the fire. "These are milkweeds. Jenny, if you'll boil these,

I'll go back and get the other stuff."

"Didn't Mom give us milkweed before?" Rick was making a face.

"Yeah," I said, "and it wasn't half bad. What else have you got?"

"Wild carrot, cattails, and pigweed."

"Pigweed? Oh, retch!"

"Shut up, Rick. You've never even tasted it."

"But pigweed?"

"It's also called lamb's quarters. I have a book that says it makes the best boiled greens you can get. Better than spinach, even."

"Wouldn't take much to be better than spinach," Rick said.

"Do I boil these whole plants?" I asked Marcia. She'd brought them, roots and all.

"Just the smaller leaves on the top, and those flower buds that haven't opened yet."

"I just boil them?"

"Right. Use river water."

Ben had gone off to catch more fish, so I put some bigger sticks on the fire and went down to the river to fill the kettle. Then I pulled the smallest leaves off the plants, trying to ignore the sticky white sap that oozed out of them and dropped them into the kettle, along with the flowers that were still buds. They sort of reminded me of broccoli. It made them seem more like food and less like weeds. Then I tried putting the kettle on the fire. First I rested it on a couple of the larger pieces of wood, but no sooner had I gotten it balanced so it wouldn't spill, than one of the pieces of wood shifted. If I hadn't grabbed fast, the whole kettle would have turned over.

Rick had been watching this. "You have to find two forked sticks," he said.

"Forked sticks? What for?"

"We studied the Pilgrims in social studies last year. They stuck forked sticks in the ground, one on each side of the fire, and then they put another stick across and hung the kettle from that. I saw a picture."

"Well, don't just stand there. Take the hatchet and find some forked sticks."

He did, and we got them jammed into the soft ground. Then he found a long, straight stick to lay across the top. I tried hanging the kettle from that. It worked. And it was just the right distance above the fire, too. I put on more wood so the water would boil.

Marcia came back with her arms loaded down with cattails. "Jenny, would you cut the shoots off of these?"

"What are shoots?"

"The bottoms—where they're still white or just beginning to get green."

"And throw them away?"

"No. The shoots are what we're going to eat. Throw away the leaves."

"Mom gives us cattail tubers."

"I know, but I don't have anything to dig them out with. Shoots are edible, too. My book says they're called Cossack asparagus. Just take the part where young leaves are starting to form. Peel off that tough outside part."

"Do they taste like asparagus?" Rick asked, making a face.

"How should I know? I've never tried them before."

"We should make hollandaise sauce," I said, my mouth watering at the thought.

"Salt will have to do. I'm going back to get the pigweed."

"Call it that other name," Rick said.

"Okay. Lamb's quarters. Be right back."

The water was boiling by this time, and the milkweed leaves and flower buds had turned a really vibrant green. "That doesn't look half bad," I said.

"Yuck," Rick said. When I looked around a few minutes later, he was gone again. His backpack was gone, too. I wondered if he was carrying toilet paper in his pack or what.

"I got another one!" Ben shouted from near the river. "Can we manage on two fish?"

"How big?"

"This one's even bigger than the other one."

His first catch had looked decent-sized to me. I didn't think I'd want to eat all of it. With just three of us eating fish, that one and a bigger one ought to be enough. "Unless you can catch another one in about three minutes, let's go with two. I'm dying over here. I want to eat!"

"Okay. I have to clean them, though."

"Fine. Just hurry up."

Ben came back and got his knife. "Won't take long. Hey, Rick! You want to help me clean the fish?"

"You mean wash them?" Rick's voice, from the bushes, was muffled again.

"No, I mean cut their heads off and clean the guts out."

"Are you nuts?"

Ben laughed. "Okay, okay." He went back down to the river, and I cut up the cattails. Marcia came back with her arms full of greenery. It all looked just like weeds to me. "You sure that stuff's better than spinach?"

"The book says so."

"You said wild carrots."

"That's what these things here are."

"That's Queen Anne's lace. Even I know that."

"Also called wild carrot."

"I don't see any carrots."

"These are the tops. This year's roots aren't big enough, and last year's are too big. They'd be all woody."

"So what are we supposed to eat?"

"You peel the stems and boil them. They're supposed to taste like carrots."

"I wish there was something that tasted like potatoes," I said.

"The Pilgrims used something for potatoes, but I haven't seen any. All I have are these black-and-white drawings to go on." Marcia held out the little paperback handbook she was using. "I just got the ones I was sure of."

I thought of us all dying out there in the wilderness from eating some poisonous weed Marcia had mistaken for something else. "You're sure you're sure of these?"

"Of course."

"Good." I knew better than to quibble with Marcia. "So, what do we do next? The milkweed's probably ready."

"Let's cook the cattails next. Has Ben got the fish ready to cook? We don't have enough pans to do everything at once."

"He's cleaning them now. We can use the frying pan for them, can't we?"

"I think you can put them on sticks and roast them like hot dogs, too," Marcia said.

She went down to the river to wash the greens, while I dumped the cooked milkweed out on a plate. I hoped it wouldn't taste worse cold. Then I got more water and put the cattails in to boil. I shook a little salt into the water. I couldn't help thinking the whole meal would be a lot better if we had butter along.

Next we boiled the peeled carrot stems. They were skinny little green things and looked ridiculous in the pan. By the time those were tender and Marcia said they were done, we were nearly out of firewood. I couldn't believe how much wood it took to keep a fire going ferociously enough to cook with. I sent Rick off to get more.

A few minutes later, Ben came up with his fish. He didn't look so triumphant anymore.

"What happened to the fish?" I asked. "I thought you said the second was bigger than the first."

"It was."

"So where is it?"

"It's this one." He pointed to a whitish gray bit of fish about three inches long. "By the time you take off the head and the tail and the fins, there isn't as much as I thought there would be." The other piece was even smaller.

"Didn't that happen to you before?"

He shrugged. "It was only me then," he said, and dumped the fish into the frying pan. "We have any oil or anything?"

"No," Marcia said. "Couldn't we roast them on sticks?"

"I'd rather do them in a pan."

"Okay, the fish are your part, you fix them."

If you've ever been camping, you probably know about campfire smoke. It doesn't just drift cozily upward the way you see it in pictures. It wafts. Sideways. In the general direction of any human being who happens to get near. In this case, since I was the one dealing with the kettle, it wafted at me. It is impossible to put a kettle on a fire, or stir it, with your back turned. By the time Rick got back with more wood, I thought I was going blind. My eyes burned and everything looked blurry. I let Marcia put the new wood on the fire while I got away from the smoke for a while. Then, squinting so that I could barely see through my eyelashes, I put the kettle full of wet pigweed leaves on the crossbar. Ten seconds later the crossbar broke, dumping the kettle and pigweed into the fire. Luckily, it didn't put the fire out. But even if we'd wanted more than anything in the world to eat pigweed, we'd have been out of luck. What wasn't smoldering right in the fire was covered in ashes and dirt.

The sun was getting low in the sky by now, and my stomach had set up such a commotion I thought I could probably be heard on the other side of the mountain. The mosquitoes were out with a vengeance and didn't seem to mind the campfire smoke at all. While Ben cooked the fish, the rest of us slathered insect repellent all over ourselves.

Finally Ben announced the fish was done. It was time to eat our survival dinner. I had to admit, it smelled pretty good. Just like real food. Rick had disappeared again. I started to worry. I figured he must be sick, to have to go off into the bushes that often. So this time, instead of calling to him, I went into the bushes after him. His health was more important, I thought, than his modesty.

What I found was not a sick child. What I found was Rick Skinner sitting on a rock, surrounded by bushes, stuffing an Oreo cookie into his mouth.

"Richard Skinner, what are you doing?"

He was so startled, he almost choked. "Mmmf argle mmmf," was about what he said.

"Where'd you get those?" I asked, and snatched up his backpack. Inside it was about two-thirds of one of those giant packages and a whole lot of dark brown crumbs. "You rat! You've eaten a ton of them!"

Rick swallowed. "Well, I don't like weeds!"

"You think the rest of us are crazy about them?"

"You can eat them, at least."

"Yeah, and we're going to eat Oreos, too. Does Mom know you took these?"

He shook his head. I'd have been madder at him, but mostly I was glad I'd found the cookies. I stuffed one into my own mouth. It tasted better than anything I'd eaten in my whole life. "From now on, we share these," I said. "Even steven."

And it's a good thing, too. Ben's fish, which had gotten even littler in the cooking, had also stuck to the pan. I don't think anybody got more than three mouthfuls of it. It didn't taste bad, though. I even sort of wished there was more. The cattails, with lots of salt, weren't awful. They didn't taste like asparagus, but they didn't make anybody sick or anything. Rick, of course, didn't taste them.

Marcia was the first to take a bite of the milkweed. Bite, chew, gag, splutter, spit. Then spit, spit, spit. "Oh, ugh, ugh, ugh, give me some water. Quick!"

Ben handed her his canteen, which was running dangerously low. She took one mouthful, rinsed it around like mouthwash, and spit it out. Then she finished the rest. "Oh, ugh!" she said again. "What did you do to that stuff?"

"I just did what you told me to. I boiled it."

"You mean you put it in boiling water, right?"

"No, I mean I put it in water and boiled it." I didn't think it was fair to grump at me. It wasn't my idea to eat weeds in the first place.

"Oh, rats, I forgot to warn you. You have to boil the water first and then drop the milkweed in. If you put it in cold water and then boil it, you set the bitter taste all the way through it!"

"So much for milkweed." Ben dumped the rest out on the ground. "Who's willing to try the carrot stems first?"

Marcia finally had to be the one. She was the expert, after all. She put plenty of salt on before she even tried. "Edible," she said. Then, "Carroty, but edible."

The Oreos saved us. We saved four each for the morning and ate all the rest. Then we put the last of the wood on the fire. The sun had gone down by this time, and the only light came from the fire. It flickered and danced and threw strangely shaped shadows on the ground.

Rick, who'd been sitting off by himself while the rest of us ate, scooched over and sat very close to me. "Do we know there aren't any bears around here?" he asked.

"No bears," Ben said.

"It's awful dark here now," Rick said, and scooched even closer to me.

I put my arm around him. "We've got flashlights and our fire," I said.

"But we're out of wood."

"When the fire gets low, we'll just snuggle down in our sleeping bags and go to sleep."

"I like it better in *Brunhilda*," Rick said. "I wish Buffy was here. Why did Mom and Dad make us come out here?"

"So we would learn to cooperate with each other," Marcia said.

"I think they had another reason, too," I said.

"What other reason?" This was Ben.

"Well, you know how small *Brunhilda* is." They all nodded. I could see nobody else had thought of this. "Look, you guys, we have been on the road for a long time now."

"So?"

"So, Mom and Dad have had about as much privacy since we left home as a pair of goldfish in a bowl."

"So?"

This was Rick. Ben and Marcia had already caught on.

"So they wanted one night alone."

"You mean they sent us out where we could get eaten by bears just so they could have *Brunhilda* to themselves?"

I patted Rick's shoulder. "We're not going to be eaten by bears. This is a state park and we're fine, and anyway we've got Ben, and he knows how to survive in the wilderness."

Ben cleared his throat. "Um. Jenny—um—"

"What?"

"Listen, will you guys promise—*promise*—not to tell Mom and Dad if I tell you something?"

I looked over at Marcia. She shrugged and nodded. Rick nodded, too. "Okay, we promise."

"And swear on your dead ancestors' graves?"

"We solemnly swear."

"Okay, then. I don't really know how to survive in the wilderness."

"Of course you do. For a few days anyway."

"Nope."

"But you were gone all that time."

"I know. And if I'd been out a few more hours, I'd have died of starvation or cold or something."

"Cold? Starvation? What are you talking about?"

"Well, for one thing, I didn't take matches—I took flint and steel."

"Flint and steel, just like the Pilgrims," Rick said.

"Yeah, well, I'm not a Pilgrim."

"Didn't you get a fire started?" Marcia asked.

"A fire? I could barely even get sparks. And when I did, they wouldn't go where I wanted them to. They were supposed to fall on the tinder and start it smoldering, and then I was supposed to very carefully and very gently blow on the tinder until it flamed up. Well, the sparks just went off sideways and disappeared."

"So, how'd you cook your fish?"

"I didn't."

"Ben, you ate raw fish?"

"I didn't even catch any fish."

"Not even one?" Rick had pulled away from me now and was sitting straight up. "Why not?"

"I didn't take any fish hooks. Sam Gribley didn't take hooks, so I didn't either. He sharpened one twig and tied it to another one to make a hook."

"Why didn't you do that?"

"I tried. I tried and I tried and I tried. If I could get them to stay together long enough to get the line attached, they came apart when I tried to put a worm on."

"One of my plant books says you can make fish hooks out of the thorns from a hawthorne tree," Marcia said.

"Well, I don't know what a hawthorne tree looks like," Ben said. "And, anyway, that isn't how Sam did it, so I didn't know about thorns."

"Do you mean you didn't have anything to eat the whole time you were gone?"

"Nope. Some survival trip that was." In the flickering light from the fire, Ben looked very sad for a moment, and then he grinned. "But you know what? Mom and Dad were right about the Outward Bound Experience."

"How were they right?" Rick wasn't ready to forgive them for sending us out without food into possible bear country.

"They wanted us to cooperate with each other, and that's what we've done. Marcia got the vegetables . . . "

"Ugh."

"Jenny had the idea for the fishing reel—I'd never have caught a fish without that."

"I didn't do anything, though," Rick said. "I'm not any good at anything."

"You brought the Oreos!" Ben said.

"And you knew about how to hang a kettle over the fire, too. I didn't know that."

Rick grinned. "I did, didn't I. I helped. And without the Oreos, we'd have starved."

We sat for a little while longer, watching the fire die down to glowing embers. Crickets and frogs were singing all around us, and the river made comfortable noises over its rocks. The bugs had mostly gone when it got dark. Mom and Dad's plan had worked in more ways than one. Here we were, sitting around a fire we'd built, in our own campsite, after a dinner we mostly found and made all by ourselves. It felt pretty great. I hoped they were having as much fun as we were.

......The Final Quest......

The campfire part was fun, it really was. But the rest of
the night wasn't. At least for me. As far as I could tell, the
others went to sleep about ten seconds after they crawled
into their sleeping bags. Not me. First of all, there were
bumps under me. It felt as if we'd pitched the tent on a
gravel pit. No, make that a rock quarry. The bumps were
much bigger than gravel. First I tried sleeping on my side.
That doesn't work at all. On your side you have a shoulder
and a hip that both need places to be—indentations or
something. When those bony places are on hard ground,
there's no way to be comfortable. Then I tried lying on my
stomach. I felt the bumps worse that way. Then I lay on
my back, and even though that wasn't comfortable, it was
better. Because we didn't have pillows, I bunched my jacket
up under my head. Jackets make lousy pillows.

Then there were the sounds. When all four of us were
sitting together around the campfire, the night sounds were
pretty. Cozy. Comforting. Crickets, frogs, water gurgling—
all very pleasant. The minute I was settled with my sleeping
bag up to my chin, a whole bunch of new sounds started.
There were ominous cracklings and snappings. These
could have been caused by bears wandering around in the
underbrush or slashers trying to sneak up on the campsite.
Then there were eerie moaning sounds. I tried to think of

sane, rational sources for these sounds—wind, maybe, or trees rubbing together, or even a rare species of owl calling to one another. The trouble was, I kept thinking of Mirkwood. And goblins. Or trolls. Or ring-wraiths.

I pulled my sleeping bag up over my head and risked suffocation because the sounds weren't so loud that way. I must have fallen asleep eventually, because suddenly I was tied hand and foot at the bottom of a mine shaft into which feathers were falling like snow. They fell more and more thickly, covering my eyes and nose and mouth so that I couldn't breathe. I was trying to pull my hands free to brush them off my face, when Rick started yelling at me to leave his cookies alone. I blinked and was awake—in the tent, my sleeping bag still over my face and wrapped tightly around me, and Rick really yelling about cookies.

I stuck my head into the air. Marcia was sitting up in her sleeping bag with her flashlight on. "What's the matter, Rick?" she shouted.

"Go on, get out of here, go away!" Rick yelled.

"What is it?" I called. "What's out there!"

"Stupid skunk," Rick yelled. "Stupid, stupid—"

"Did you say skunk?" I scrambled out of my sleeping bag and grabbed my flashlight. "Don't move, Rick. Don't scare it."

When I got my head out of the tent, there was Rick, aiming his flashlight beam at the retreating back and tail of a skunk. "Stupid skunk," Rick said. "Stupid, stupid . . ."

Ben crawled out of their tent. "What happened?"

Rick sniffed. "I heard noises, so I came out to see what it was, and that stupid skunk was eating our cookies. Somebody left the bag on that rock, and the skunk got it down. He tore it open and was eating and eating. I tried to scare him away, but he just sat there and watched me with his awful red eyes until he had finished the very last one. And then he stomped up and down on the empty bag!"

"You're lucky," Ben said. "We're all lucky."

"Lucky? Now we don't have any breakfast!"

"Yeah, well, we could all have been sprayed with skunk spray, too."

"I should have thrown something at it," Rick grumped.

"You should not. Don't you ever, ever throw anything at a skunk, I don't care what it's doing."

"Stupid skunk."

We finally got Rick calmed down and back to bed. It was amazing. We'd found an animal Rick didn't like. The last thing I was aware of, once I was snuggled back into my sleeping bag, was Rick calling the skunk names.

When I opened my eyes it was light out and I smelled woodsmoke and the astonishingly wonderful aroma of frying fish. I crawled out to see what was going on, and there, bent over the fire, was Ben with a full frying pan. He'd gotten up before dawn and gone fishing. This time he'd caught three decent-sized bluegill and a catfish. He'd also remembered that you can cover the bottom of a frying pan with salt if you don't have grease, and what you're cooking won't stick as badly. The sun was shining, and the chilly morning air was beginning to warm up.

"Gorgeous day," I said, and took a deep breath. The smoke and fish smells were gorgeous, too.

"Get the others up. Breakfast is nearly ready. I wish we had some cocoa or something—I've got some water boiling."

Marcia appeared at the entrance to our tent. "I know where there's some sassafras. We can have sassafras tea."

And so the four Skinner children, cooperating, independent, hardy Outward Bound souls, had a wilderness breakfast of fish and sassafras tea. Even Rick discovered that with salt and pepper, he could eat catfish. "It's almost good," he admitted. Probably he was just too hungry to hold out. We all liked the tea. Rick insisted on taking some sassafras root home with us when we broke camp.

Ben scouted around while the rest of us packed up the tents and cleaned the dishes as well as we could in hot river water. He finally found the trail we should have taken the day before. It turned out to be the one the tree had fallen across—something that must have happened in the rain. Anyway, the hike back to the campground was a lot easier, since we didn't have to get through the bog.

We got back just before noon. Mom and Dad were sitting outside *Brunhilda* on lawn chairs, basking in the sun. When we'd finished telling the whole story (except about the skunk and the cookies), Mom fixed us a huge and delicious lunch of peanut butter and jelly sandwiches and milk.

"I thought I bought one of those enormous packages of Oreos," she said when we'd finished, "but I couldn't find it." We looked at Rick. He pretended not to notice. "We can stop and get some ice cream on the way."

"On the way where?" I had visions of another Orville Corners. "We're not looking for another village green, are we?"

"No village greens," Dad said. "No little towns. We're going to go visit an old Adirondack Mountain craftsman."

"You mean like those kids in the *Foxfire* book did? Can I take my tape recorder and ask him questions? What does he make?" Marcia, having had enough of edible wild plants, was ready for a new project.

"He makes rocking chairs, and, yes, you can take your tape recorder. That's the whole point. He's almost the last of his kind. An old man who lives alone up in the mountains, raises his own food, and makes these chairs in the old-fashioned way that's been handed down in his family for generations. Except that he's the last of the line. His chairs are the last ones. He brings them down to the store on the back of his mule."

"What store?" Ben asked.

"A wonderful old trading post. Your mother and I found it, just outside the park. The store sells all sorts of odds and ends along with this old craftsman's rocking chairs. We're going to drive over there on our way out to pick up the one I bought and get directions to the old man's cabin."

Ben looked around *Brunhilda*'s main living space. "Where do you intend to put a rocking chair?"

"We'll tie it on the roof."

"Then where are we going?" I asked. The truth was, I didn't much feel like being on the road again. I hadn't even had time to investigate the beach where we were.

"We need to talk about that. Your mother and I thought maybe we should just find a nice place we all like and settle down for a while."

"You mean not travel anymore? Just stay in one place?" Ben looked doubtful.

Ever practical, Marcia wanted to know where we'd stay. Rick voted to go back to the park in Pennsylvania where he could be a Junior Ranger again.

"We've been going over the travel books, and there are

some nice-looking campgrounds in the Adirondacks—some of them combine wilderness with some of the amenities of civilization."

"Does amenities mean food?" Rick asked.

"Certainly food," Mom assured him. "What do you think?"

Marcia nodded. Me, too. Then Rick.

"Wilderness?" Ben asked. "Will I be able to fish?"

"All you want," Dad said.

And so it was agreed. As soon as we'd visited with Dad's mountain craftsman, we would find a place to settle. We packed up again and left (after emptying *Brunhilda*'s waste tanks and filling up with water). This time the packing wasn't even very hard to do. It's all a matter of practice.

Marcia's and my room felt like a palace after the two-person tent. And my bed—well, in spite of the clothing lumps, it was like lying on a cloud. After most of a night of listening to ominous sounds and imagining massacres, I would have gone right to sleep if we hadn't gotten to the trading post so quickly. In no time, we were pulling in to the rutted, gravel parking lot of the weirdest store I'd ever seen in my life. As soon as Dad stopped, a short, broad-shouldered man with long gray hair pulled back in a pony-tail and a huge, drooping mustache rushed out the door of the crumbling log cabin, whose sign claimed it to be ISAIAH'S ADIRONDACK TRADING POST. He wove his way through the rusting lawn mowers, tractor parts, concrete birdbaths, animal statues, and warped furniture that lit-tered the muddy grass between the porch and the parking lot.

"Hello, hello, hello," he was shouting as he came. "Glad to see you. It sure took you long enough. Began to think you weren't coming. Never mind, just come on in. Glad to have you here finally!"

He kept this up as he hurried toward *Brunhilda*. This was the warmest welcome we'd had since the trip began. I went up to the front room so I could see and hear better. Maybe Dad was right about real people after all.

Dad got out and went to meet the man, his hand held out. But as he got closer and closer, the man's expression changed. By the time he and Dad were face-to-face, the guy refused to shake hands. "Aren't you the one bought that chair yesterday?" he asked.

Dad dropped his hand a little awkwardly. "Yes. I said I'd be by to pick it up today. . . ."

"Oh, I get it. You came by yesterday to scout me out, right? And you bought a chair so I wouldn't suspect. So where's Kuralt? And where're the TV cameras?"

"Excuse me? Did you said Kuralt?"

"It's about time, you know. I must 'a sent you twenty letters. Thirty, maybe. When's he coming?"

"Do you mean Charles Kuralt?"

"When's he gonna get here?"

Dad cleared his throat and shook his head. "There must be some mistake. I've never even met Charles Kuralt."

The man's eyes got very squinty. "You mean you didn't come here 'cause of all those letters I sent? You didn't come to do a story about my trading post for 'On the Road'? You aren't putting me on TV?"

"I'm sorry, no. I just came to pick up the chair I bought yesterday and to get directions."

The man stamped one orange leather boot into the gravel. "Well, I'm sick and tired, do you hear? People comin' by in these big bus things all the time, and not one of 'em—*not one*—turns out to be Kuralt. Where is he, that's what I want to know. Where is he?"

"I'm sure I don't—"

"And how come nobody answers my letters? Tell me that!"

"I don't know. I just . . ."

The man turned his back and started back toward the store. "I know, I know, you just came for your chair."

"And directions," Dad said.

The man stopped and looked over his shoulder. "To where?"

"You remember I asked you yesterday about the man who makes the rocking chairs. I wanted to find out how to get to his place. We want to meet him."

"You want to meet 'im, huh?" He went back to threading his way among the junk. "I guess I can give directions to his place 'bout as well as anybody." He chuckled. " 'Bout as well as anybody."

Ben helped Dad get the wood and cane rocking chair onto the roof. It didn't look like something I wanted to sit in. "Not very user-friendly" is what Ben whispered to me, as he climbed the ladder to the roof. It was rustic, though, whatever else. Once it was securely roped to the luggage rack, Dad took a road map and went inside with Isaiah to get the directions.

"Okay, guys," he said, when he'd buckled himself into the driver's seat again. "Let's get back on the road."

"Sure thing, Charley," Mom said.

"That guy's been trying to get Kuralt out here for ten years. Every time he sees a motor home, he thinks he's about to be a TV star!"

"This close to a state park, he must have a lot of false alarms," Marcia said.

"Probably not that many," Ben said. "I'll bet people don't exactly flock to his door to buy his wares."

"He has some nice things," Dad protested.

"Yeah, like the rocker." Ben did not sound sincere.

Mom made Dad stop at the first grocery store we came to so we could stock up on food. "Those directions don't look as if they'll take us past many metropolitan centers," she said.

She was right. The grocery store where we stopped—in a town so tiny it wasn't much more than the grocery and a gas station—was the last one we saw. Every time Dad took a turn he was supposed to take, the road got smaller, until *Brunhilda* stretched practically from one side to the other. Since it was also up and down and up and down and very curvy, Dad took to blowing his horn a lot to warn cars that might be coming toward us. But there never were any. Finally, late in the afternoon, we came to a place where the gravel road we were on ended in a fork. Neither possibility looked inviting because neither seemed to be a real road. They were just wheel ruts with grass growing in between. And where the road we were on at least had gravel between the mud puddles, the wheel ruts were nothing but mud and an occasional wicked-looking rock.

"What now?" Mom asked. "Should we turn around?"

Dad just looked at her. Turning *Brunhilda* around on this road, with trees and bushes practically brushing her sides, was not something even a stunt driver would be able to accomplish.

"What do the directions say?"

Dad shook his head. "They don't. For the last few miles there has been no resemblance whatsoever between these directions and this road. There was supposed to be a road going off to the left about two miles back."

"There wasn't," Mom said.

"I'm aware of that, Eleanor. That's why I kept going."

"Maybe the left fork is what he meant."

"He didn't call it a fork. It's supposed to be one road. Off to the left."

"Well, if we can't turn around, we have to choose one of these, don't we?"

"That or back out eight or ten miles."

"We could toss a coin." This was Marcia's suggestion.

"I'd like to base my choice on something a little more reasonable than a coin toss," Dad said.

"Like what?" Mom asked. "That crazy man's directions?"

"I could go scout ahead," Ben offered. "I'm good at that."

"I'll take the left fork," Dad said. "That must be what he meant. He did say left."

And so we started down the two wheel ruts to the left. Trees and bushes scraped and slapped at us as we went, and every so often, we skidded sideways in the mud. *Brunhilda* bounced and bucked and bottomed out about twice a minute. I was glad the refrigerator was full of plastic containers. Chatter, who'd finally become accustomed to *Brunhilda* on the move, began to yowl again, and I hurried her back into our room. I was practically bruised and bloody from bouncing into counters and walls by the time I got back to the couch. Just then Dad let out a yowl that rivaled Chatter's.

Brunhilda came to a sudden, shuddering halt. Ben ended up on the floor next to the dinette.

I will not repeat Dad's next words. Or Mom's either, for that matter. In front of us, completely across what there was of the road, was what amounted to a trench—more than a foot deep.

"Now we'll *have* to back out," Mom said.

"Obviously," Dad said through clenched teeth.

He changed gears and pressed on the accelerator. *Brunhilda* groaned, but didn't move. "Rats!" Dad said. He tried again. This time she groaned a little louder, shuddered, and slipped sideways slightly.

"Are we stuck?" Rick asked. Marcia clapped her hand over his mouth, but not in time.

"Of course we're stuck!" Dad roared. "Do you feel us going anywhere?"

"Can you rock it?" Mom asked.

"I'll have to try."

Dad put *Brunhilda* in forward and pressed on the gas. She bucked a little, and he changed gears quickly. She slipped sideways slightly, and he threw her into forward again. There was another groan, another shudder, and then suddenly *Brunhilda* seemed to leap forward. There was a jolt, a lurch, a horrendous, sickening crunch of a noise, and then silence. *Brunhilda*'s floor slanted slightly downward in the front and slightly to the left.

No one said anything for a moment. And no one moved. Not even Buffy. Dad sat with his elbows on the steering wheel and his head in his hands. Finally, Mom broke the silence.

"Michael?"

"Yes, Eleanor?"

"What do you think it was?"

"The axle."

"Oh."

"Yes."

Mom took a deep breath, and then she turned around to look at all of us. She put on a decent imitation of a smile. "Well, kids, it looks as if we've found a place to spend the night."

.... Planted ....

It was the axle, all right. Broken. There was no way we could go anywhere, forward or back. We couldn't even get *Brunhilda* level. Her left front wheel was in the trench, sort of dangling in the air, and her middle was planted firmly on the rock that had broken the axle.

We all stood outside *Brunhilda*, looking at her. It was a sickening, hopeless feeling. If she'd been a horse, we'd have had to shoot her. Buffy, oblivious to catastrophe, was off frolicking in the woods; Chatter had gone off to murder something small and furry; Czar Nicholas, refusing to budge from his now-crippled home, sat curled on the back of the sofa, waiting patiently for dinner to be served. The image that kept coming to my mind was from "Gilligan's Island." We were shipwrecked. And while we were surrounded by land rather than ocean, the effect was just about the same. We hadn't seen so much as a house for miles and miles.

"This road has to lead somewhere," Mom said. "To a house, at least. Someplace with a phone."

"With our luck, this road leads to an abandoned mine," Dad said.

"I'll scout ahead," Ben offered. This time Dad accepted his offer. There wasn't a lot else to do.

"Can I go with you?" Rick asked. "I've never seen an abandoned mine. I've never seen a mine at all."

"Sure. Come on. What do we do if we find a phone? Call Triple A?"

Dad ran his hand through his hair and sighed. "I guess. Even this godforsaken piece of mountain must have a Triple A garage somewhere." He pulled out his wallet. "Take the card so you can give them our membership number."

"How will I tell them where we are?"

"The last road we were on that had a name was a county road—73."

"What county?"

"How should I know? Just tell them we're about ten miles north of County Road 73 on a dirt road with no name."

So Rick and Ben stepped down into the trench, clambered up the other side, and set off following the wheel ruts. Ben whistled and Buffy joined them, running off first one way and then the other, barking joyfully.

"Could we jack up this side?" Mom asked. "At least get the floor level?"

Dad looked into the trench. "The only thing solid enough to count on is that rock she's already resting on. We'd better leave well enough alone."

"Well"—Mom was determined to be plucky and cheerful—"it's a good thing she's a motor home instead of a plain car. At least we have everything we need. Come on, girls, let's go get dinner started."

We were used to living in *Brunhilda* now, cooking in the tiny galley, even showering without using more than ten tablespoons of water. But now it all took on a new slant, if you'll pardon the expression. Marcia went to set the table and the dishes slid off. Mom had to hold the pan on the

stove while she browned the hamburger for spaghetti
sauce. Then, when she went to boil water for the pasta,
there was more trouble. When she set the kettle full of
water on the stove, it started to spill, so she had to empty
some of the water out. I stood next to the stove with a hot
pad in my hand, holding the kettle in place the whole time
the pasta was cooking, so we didn't have to worry about
the kettle slipping off and scalding anyone. Marcia fixed
the salad by sitting on the lower side of the dinette and
leaning against the table as she chopped. Anything that
slid down stopped at her chest.

While we were fixing dinner, thumping and clumping
from the back end of *Brunhilda* told us Dad was climbing
up onto the roof. "I wonder what he wants from up there,"
Mom was saying, when Dad's voice boomed down at us.

"Ye gods and little fishies!"

"What, dear?" Mom shouted. "What's the matter?"

There followed another string of words I can't print here.
And more bumping.

"What's the matter?" Mom shouted again.

The rocking chair appeared in the galley window, bouncing gently against *Brunhilda*'s side as it was lowered on
the rope that had tied it to the roof. "This chair!" Dad yelled.
"This wonderful, handmade chair. The reason we are out
here in this godforsaken wilderness, on a wild goose chase
to find a mythical craftsman!"

"What are you talking about?"

"Made in Taiwan!" Dad roared. The chair continued
downward until it bumped onto the ground. "Stamped on
the underside of the seat. 'Made in Taiwan,' it says. There
is no Adirondack Mountains craftsman. He doesn't exist."

More thumping followed as Dad climbed back down. He

stuck his head in the door. "That madman who wanted me to be Charles Kuralt made the whole story up. Methods passed down for generations. The last of his line. Brought down to the store on muleback. That crook! That con man! No wonder CBS has ignored his letters. He's a total fraud."

"What about the map?" Marcia asked, chopping a green onion, whose pieces rolled down the table and into the bowl she'd put in her lap.

"Heaven only knows where he intended to send us," Dad said.

"He must have made up this last bit," Mom said. "The map didn't fit the road anymore."

"I should have known. I should have known. He's back in that rats' nest of a store right now laughing his head off." Dad withdrew. I had a feeling he wanted to be alone.

When dinner was ready, Ben and Rick weren't back and the sun was going down. I went outside to see what Dad was doing. He was sitting in the fraudulent rocking chair, staring at *Brunhilda*'s crippled front end. His face was a picture of misery. "They're not back yet, huh?" I asked.

"If it gets dark and they're not here, I'll take a lantern and go after them."

"Anything I can do?"

Dad shook his head. "This wasn't such a good idea, this Getaway, Jenny."

Dad looked really awful. His fantasies had crumbled under the heavy burden of reality. "Real people" weren't one bit nicer than "city people"; the "Camping Fraternity" turned out to have nothing in common with Dad except their motor homes; and his old-fashioned, pioneering craftsman was really a factory in Taiwan.

"I've brought my whole family into the wilderness and

stranded them here. Beginning to end, this trip has been an unmitigated disaster."

"Don't say that," I said. "I've had fun. Lots of fun."

Marcia joined us. "Me, too. All of us have."

"I haven't," Dad said. If he'd been Rick's age, I'd have expected the tears to start, his voice sounded so pathetic.

"Don't be silly, Michael," Mom said, joining us. "It's been an adventure, and you know it. Besides, we'd planned to stop moving anyway. Why not now?"

"Because we are at the tail end of nowhere, that's why."

Just then we heard Buffy barking. The sound came not from ahead of us, where we'd have expected it, but from behind.

"We're back! We're back!" This was Rick.

Soon Rick and Ben and Buffy appeared on the road behind *Brunhilda*. "There wasn't any mine," Rick complained.

"And there wasn't any house either," Ben said. "No phone. No nothing. It wouldn't have mattered which fork we took back there, because the road's nothing but a great big circle. If we'd gone right instead of left, we'd be in the same position except that we'd be stuck on the other side of the trench instead of here."

"Now what?" Marcia asked.

"Now dinner," Mom said. "Tomorrow we'll find a house and a phone and get out of here." She was using her plucky voice again.

"I heard a dog bark," Ben said. "Buffy started toward it, but came back. I think it scared her off. Tomorrow I want to try looking in that direction, because a dog must mean people."

Dad was in no mood to be optimistic or plucky. "Probably

a feral dog. Probably a dog pack. We'd better all go together."

"Meantime," Mom said, "dinner."

And so, holding our plates in place, we managed to eat. Then we cleaned up and got ready for bed. When I opened the bin over my bed to get out my hairbrush, everything came flying out on top of me. Other than that, the rest of the evening was uneventful. Oh, yes, except that Chatter returned with her usual love offering. This time Rick couldn't moan and groan over which particular cute furry animal had been sent to furry animal heaven, because all Chatter brought back was its liver, which she deposited in Dad's lap.

After breakfast the next morning, we all set off down the road to see if we could find any sign of human habitation. "If worst comes to worst," Mom said, "we just retrace our steps till we get back to civilization. It can't be more than ten or fifteen miles."

"Right," said Dad. "Ten or fifteen miles up and down and up and down."

It was true. We were in the mountains. People in the Himalayas or the Alps—even the Rockies—might not call the Adirondacks "real" mountains. But they were real enough for us.

We'd walked for nearly half an hour and were taking a rest, when we heard the dog barking. The sound came from the hillside up to our right, but the trees and brush were so dense we couldn't see anything. Buffy's fur rose along her back, but she didn't head off toward the other dog.

"I think it scared her last night," Ben said. "She ran off, all excited, but she came right back."

"Let's go," Dad said. "Everybody stay behind me in case

it's a wild dog." He headed off through the undergrowth. "And watch out for poison ivy."

The dog continued to bark, and we got closer and closer to the sound. Buffy lagged far behind. Suddenly, Dad stopped. Ben, who was right behind him, crashed into his back, and Mom crashed into Ben.

"Not another step." The voice was low and gravelly and menacing.

I couldn't see anything because Mom and Dad and Ben were in the way.

"Who's that?" Rick asked, as he and Marcia came up next to me.

"Shh. I can't see," I whispered.

"That's enough, Lucifer!" the voice shouted, and the dog stopped barking.

"Excuse me, ma'am," Dad said. "We're looking for a phone."

"You're going to look a long time up here. And still you won't find one."

"Is this your place?" Dad asked.

"You think I'd be defending somebody else's?"

Rick pushed past me and through the tangle of weeds and vines until he was next to Dad. Dad put his hand out to stop him. Marcia and I followed.

The source of the voice was a woman. An old, old, old woman. Her face was more crinkled and wrinkly than the dried apple puppet I'd made in third grade. Her hair was white and pulled back in a bun, but sort of wispy around her face. She was wearing a plaid flannel shirt and faded denim overalls, rolled up halfway to her knees. Beneath the overalls her bony legs were bare, and on her feet were old, black high-top basketball shoes. In incredibly gnarled and wrinkled hands she was holding a shotgun, pointing it in Dad's general direction.

"You teach your children to trespass, do you?" she asked.

Mom stepped up next to Dad. "We didn't know we were trespassing," she said. "Our motor home broke down, and we were looking for a phone."

"So the man said. Like I said, you won't find one."

"Don't you have a phone?" Rick asked.

The old woman turned toward Rick, pointing the gun in his direction as she turned. "If I had a phone, you'd have found one already, wouldn't you?"

"Then how do you call people?" he asked.

"Never could abide stupid children," the woman said.

"Now just a minute," Mom said, and took a step forward. Dad grabbed Mom's arm.

The old woman swiveled toward Mom, pointing the gun at her now. "Go on out of here. I can't do a thing for you."

"Perhaps you could tell us where we could get help," Dad said. "Our motor home has a broken axle . . ."

"What'd you bring a motor home up in here for?" the woman asked.

"A wild goose chase, as it turned out," Dad said. "But it's here and it has a broken axle and we have to locate a garage."

"Nearest garage is ten miles off—the other side of this mountain." This could have been construed as helpful information, except for the woman's tone of voice.

"Can you tell us how to get there?" Mom asked. "We'll just have to walk."

The woman's gaze moved from Mom to Dad, to Ben, then to me and Marcia and Rick. "You hothouse specimens

walk? Ten miles? In these mountains? You'd never make
it halfway."

"We can walk ten miles," Marcia said. "We can walk
twenty. And we don't need help from people who point guns
at us!"

The woman's face crinkled even more as her expression
changed, and she lowered the muzzle of the gun until it
pointed at the ground. " 'Tisn't loaded," she said.

"Well, we didn't know that," Marcia said. "You scared us
half to death!" Dad gestured at her to shut up.

"And what do you think you did to me? Coming up on
my place out of the woods like that. You might've been
anybody. If I hadn't had old Lucifer barking to warn me,
you might have startled me right into a heart attack."

"Well, one of us could have had a heart attack, too,"
Marcia said, ignoring Dad's continuing gestures.

"Can't abide rude children either," the woman said. "Go
on now, get off my place."

"If you'll just tell us how to get to that garage . . ." Mom
said.

The old woman looked us all over again. "In spite of what
little Miss Manners here says, I don't think you'll make it
on foot." She sighed then, and set her gun, butt downward,
on the ground, leaning her weight on the muzzle. "Any of
you know how to ride?"

"A horse?" Dad asked.

"A mule."

Dad shrugged. "What's the difference?"

"Ride a mule and you'll find out soon enough. You want
to try?"

"I imagine I could."

"All right, then, come with me. But watch that dog of yours. Lucifer doesn't like competition."

The woman turned and went off on what now appeared to be a narrow path cut into the vines and weeds. She limped heavily, using the shotgun as if it were a cane. Ben grabbed Buffy's collar, and we followed.

In about a minute we came out of the woods into a clearing. In the middle was an old, silvery gray log cabin. It had a porch across the front that leaned at about the same angle as *Brunhilda*. Across the porch railings and up the roof supports grew morning glory vines covered with deep purple flowers. A big, black dog, which looked about as much Labrador retriever as Buffy was golden retriever, was chained to a post in the middle of the yard.

"It's a good thing I chained him up this morning," the woman said, patting his head as she limped past him, "or he'd have come out and chewed you all to bits."

Somehow, I doubted it. His face was mottled with gray, and his fat tail was thumping the ground behind him. Just in case, Ben stopped at the edge of the clearing and held onto Buffy.

"You just wait there," the woman said, "and don't bother anything." I wondered what she thought we'd bother. "I'll get Gabriel." She disappeared into a barn on the other side of the clearing.

Rick went up to the dog. "Hi, Lucifer," he said. The dog's tail thumped faster, but he didn't get up. Rick held out his hand, Lucifer sniffed it, and then Rick threw his arms around him. So much for the wicked Lucifer. He licked Rick's face from forehead to chin.

A gigantic black cat with a torn ear emerged from under

the porch and rubbed itself against the steps. Rick abandoned Lucifer and went over and sat on the steps. The cat leaped heavily into his lap and put its nose to Rick's.

"Careful," the woman said, as she reappeared, leading a large brown mule with a rope halter. "Caliban scratches. He hates strangers."

Caliban, whose purr could be heard where I was standing three feet away, was not scratching.

"Come on," the woman said to Dad. "The sooner you get started, the sooner I'll be rid of the lot of you. Hope you don't need a saddle, because I don't have one."

And so it was that Dad set off bareback on Gabriel the mule to follow the directions Minnie Berry (This was the woman's name) gave him to the nearest garage. The rest of us sat on Miss Berry's front porch and waited. Miss Berry took Lucifer and went off past the barn to work in her garden. Mom offered to help, but was refused. "You'd doubtless pull up half my vegetables, thinking they were weeds."

Mom bit her lip and didn't answer. "I'm certainly not going to push my help on her," she said after Miss Berry had disappeared. "Unpleasant old woman."

"She called me rude," Marcia said.

"That's not as bad as stupid." Rick was still petting Caliban, who was curled up in his lap.

"Never mind," Mom said. "We'll be out of here as soon as your father gets back."

"Why wait?" Ben asked. He was still holding Buffy at the edge of the clearing. "Let's go back to *Brunhilda*. Dad'll be gone forever."

"Good point. Let's go, kids."

"Can't I stay here with Caliban?" Rick asked.

Mom hesitated. "I'm not sure I want you to stay here by yourself," she said.

"Why?" Rick asked. "You think that old lady's a witch? Is that why she has a black cat?"

Mom shook her head. "Don't be silly, Rick. She's just a crotchety old woman. But I don't like that gun of hers."

"Oh, that's show," Marcia said. "She just uses it as a cane and to scare people—the wretched old thing."

"Hush, Marcia."

"Please, Mom, can't I stay till Dad gets back?"

"All right, Rick, if someone will stay with you."

Marcia volunteered. "I'll stay. I won't let that old battle-ax do anything to Rick."

"Marcia!"

"She called me rude. I might as well live up to it."

"You behave yourself."

"All right. I won't say anything like that to her face."

I thought Mom was still a little reluctant to leave Rick and Marcia, but she didn't want just to sit around on that rickety old porch waiting hours for Dad to come back either. "If you have any trouble, you both come right home, you hear?"

They nodded.

And so we left them. I went back and lay on an angle on my bed and wrote Sarah all about the mortal wounding of *Brunhilda*. I started telling about the old witch who lived in the woods with a black dog named after the devil and a black cat named after a monster, and the more I wrote, the better it got. Pretty soon I forgot all about Sarah and was just writing this story. Mom sat at the dinette table, her typewriter wedged against her chest, and wrote a column about road breakdowns. Ben took Buffy and his compass and went off to explore.

Rick and Marcia came back for lunch, and Ben got back, too, all excited. He'd found a stream full of fish. Trout, he was sure. As soon as he'd eaten, he took his fishing gear and went off again. He was back an hour later, complaining that he needed a fly rod and some flies. Marcia played her violin, and I realized it was the first time since we'd left home. It sounded great.

Later in the afternoon, when we thought Dad might be getting back, we left Buffy chained to a tree and went back to Miss Berry's. Lucifer didn't bark. He just thumped his tail in welcome. Miss Berry was nowhere to be seen when we came to the clearing, so we just sat down on the porch to wait. Caliban materialized immediately and plopped himself into Rick's lap. The air was filled with some kind of wonderful cooking smell.

We hadn't been there more than fifteen minutes, when Dad rode up. He stopped the mule in the middle of the clearing and slid off, landing with a bump and a groan. He rubbed his backside and groaned again. His expression was not cheerful.

"Well?" Mom asked. "What did they say?"

"Planted," Dad said. He rubbed his rear again. "Ooh, I think I'm crippled."

"Planted? Planted? Michael Skinner, what are you talking about?"

"That's what the garage man said. 'Planted.' *Brunhilda*'s not going anywhere, today, tomorrow, next week."

"Won't they come tow her?" Mom asked.

"Nobody around here has a rig big enough," Dad said. "You can't drag a motor home with a regular little tow truck."

"So what are we supposed to do? Leave her there to rot?"

"He's got a friend with a garage and a big tow rig down around Lake George. The friend might be willing to lend him the rig at the end of the season."

"When's that?"

"September."

"September? Do you mean *Brunhilda* has to sit there until September?"

"Unless you have a better idea. Henry, the man at the garage, suggests we go home. According to him, life in a motor home 'ain't livin' and it ain't campin'.' "

"We can't go home," Marcia pointed out. "Home's rented."

"That does present a small problem," Dad said.

"What to do from now till September," Mom said. "Wonderful."

"I don't know what you'll do till September," Miss Berry's voice came from behind us. She was standing in the open door to the cabin. "But what you'll do right now is put that mule in the barn and then come eat. Stew's getting cold."

........CONCLUSION........

(Don't Stop Yet)

It was a strange meal. We seemed almost too much for the small cabin. To get us all around the oak table, we had to jam her four chairs right up against each other and bring a bench that Rick and Marcia could share, plus Miss Berry's rocker from its place by the old wood stove she still used for cooking. And then we could barely move without bumping each other. It wasn't very bright inside because there was no electricity, and the cabin was lit only by kerosene lamps. Over the table hung a lamp that could be lowered to be lit and then raised again.

The stew was fantastic. There were biscuits, too, with fresh butter in a crockery bowl. And raspberry jam. And gingerbread for dessert. Until then, Rick had kept sneaking suspicious looks at Miss Berry, but one bite of the gingerbread won him over. After that, he wouldn't have cared if she did turn out to be a witch.

Inside the cabin Miss Berry didn't use her gun as a cane; she didn't use a cane at all. But her limp was so bad, she sort of hobbled around. It made me feel a little guilty that she was waiting on us. I offered to help when she brought the gingerbread to the table, but she said she'd somehow managed to live her life before I came along and could probably manage just as well now that I was there.

When we'd finished our gingerbread, Dad asked her if she'd always lived here alone. "It seems pretty isolated."

"Just exactly why I like it," Miss Berry said. She pounded one gnarled fist on the table. "I couldn't abide cars and trucks and air pollution. Jet planes flying over all the time and breaking your eardrums. Street gangs. Poisoned water. Pushy neighbors. I may be isolated, but I know what's what."

"But—well, you'll excuse me if I seem to be prying . . ."

"Why should I excuse you for prying?"

Dad was taken aback. "I mean—well, I . . ."

"Ask your question. If I want you to know the answer, I'll answer it. If not, not."

"You seem to have a little difficulty getting around, and I wondered how you manage this place on your own."

"I manage." Miss Berry patted her leg. "Touch of arthritis," she said, and held up her gnarled hand. "Here, too. Got a neighbor on up the mountain who comes by to help sometimes. He disks and harrows my garden for me in the spring. I've got plenty of vegetables planted." She frowned, and her wrinkles seemed to collapse in on each other. "Not so easy to keep the garden up this year, though. Arthritis seems to be getting worse. I'm not too proud to admit that." Then she bristled. "But I'll get along. I've lived here for seventy years, I guess I can live here yet awhile."

"Seventy years? How old are you?" Rick jumped, and I guessed Mom must have kicked him under the table. But it was too late.

"Never did like nosy children either," Miss Berry said.

Then she looked directly at Rick. "You want another piece of that gingerbread?"

Rick nodded. "Yes, please."

She put another piece on his plate. "There, now fill your mouth with that and don't ask any more impertinent questions." Then she looked at Mom and Dad. "Eighty-five last April."

Mom's face flushed pink. "I'm sorry, you didn't have to . . ."

"You wanted to know almost as much as the boy. I came here to teach when I was fifteen."

"Teach?" Marcia's voice was clearly disbelieving. "At fifteen?"

"In a one-room schoolhouse. Things were different in those days. If you finished school, you could teach. Yes, Miss Manners, I was a teacher at fifteen. Also at twenty and thirty and forty and fifty and sixty. I was an excellent teacher, I might add. Never sent one single stupid child out from that school in all the years I taught there." She glared meaningfully at Rick, who was just swallowing the last of his gingerbread.

"I'm not stupid!"

"I guess not," Miss Berry said. "You managed to get two pieces of gingerbread, didn't you? Anyway, Caliban likes you."

"Would you like us to help you clean up?" Mom asked.

"Certainly. I did the cooking. I guess you folks could do the washing up." She looked over at Ben. "You know how to split wood?"

"I never tried. I know how to use a hatchet, though."

"You're a sturdy-looking young man," she said, and Ben grinned. "If you think you can manage an ax, the woodbox needs filling. Woodpile's out behind the cabin. Take a lantern. The sun's getting low."

Ben stood up. His back was so straight he might have been a soldier at attention.

"I suppose you fish, too."

He nodded.

"If you're still around tomorrow, you could take my old gear and get some trout. It's been awhile since I tasted fresh fish."

"Sure."

"Well, don't just stand there. We need that wood!"

For the next half hour she kept us all hopping. Her cabin wasn't anywhere nearly as convenient as *Brunhilda*. She had running water—a pump at one end of the sink. But we had to heat it for dishwashing on the stove. She had no inside bathroom either, which Rick found out when he asked where it was. Mom washed dishes and Dad dried, the two of them muttering to each other the whole time. Miss Berry sat in her rocker directing Marcia and me as we put things away. She had Rick take the leftover stew outside to feed Caliban and Lucifer.

When the dishes were done and put away, and Ben had filled the woodbox, we gathered in the main room. Mom and Dad stood together, and Dad cleared his throat.

"As you know," he said to Miss Berry, "our motor home is stuck on your land, probably until September."

"If Henry said September, it will be at *least* September."

"Yes, well. It occurred to us that at the very least we should pay a storage fee."

"What would I want with money? I have all the money I need from social security, thank you very much. As long as I can stay here and raise what I need to eat."

"Actually," Mom said, "we weren't thinking of money, and it wouldn't be a storage fee, exactly. You mentioned that you were having a little difficulty keeping up with your garden."

"I manage." For the first time, Miss Berry's voice wasn't quite so harsh. I began to see where Mom and Dad were going with this.

Dad took over. "We've rented our house for the summer. If we called and explained the situation, we might be able to get the house back, but we'd rather not. We were planning to stop traveling anyway, and this is a beautiful spot. We thought perhaps you would let us stay in our motor home where it is. In return, we could help you with your garden."

Miss Berry frowned. I couldn't tell if it was my imagination or if I saw a sort of twinkle in her eyes. But when she spoke, her voice was as harsh as ever. "To be a help, somebody would have to know what he—or she—was doing."

"Our parents didn't raise any stupid children," Mom said, smiling. "We didn't either."

It wasn't my imagination this time. Miss Berry smiled, too.

Before I could even get my breath, everything was decided. We were staying. Rick was crazy about the idea. I think he was planning a whole summer of gingerbread. Ben, too, was pleased. After all, Miss Berry had asked him to catch her some fish. Dad's whole summer would be saved, of course. Miss Berry was about as real a person as anyone could want. A genuine American pioneer. And around this dilapidated old farm, Mom could rough it to her heart's content.

As we walked back to *Brunhilda* through the dark that night, I asked Marcia how she felt about the idea. "It's perfect!" she said.

"But I thought you couldn't stand Miss Berry."

"You don't have to like your research subject, you know," she said.

I should have known. Miss Berry was going to be Marcia's next Project.

As for me, I wasn't sure. No phone, no beach, no guys. On the other hand, I'd had a lot of fun working on that witch story. I was actually getting to like writing. It *was* beautiful here in the mountains, and quiet, and there was the Getaway to write about.

"What can we do about the slant?" Mom asked, as she climbed up into *Brunhilda*.

Dad followed her. "I've got some ideas about that."

"Me, too," Ben said.

The sun had set over the Adirondacks. Over *Brunhilda*. Over the Great Skinner Getaway. We settled into our beds that night, feeling good. Czar Nicholas and Chatter were curled contentedly at my feet. Buffy was in her usual place on the floor by the couch. Crickets chirped outside, and the wind rustled the leaves, making moon shadows dance on the wall. As I was drifting off to sleep, there was a noise and a jolt. My bed tipped a little more. *Brunhilda* was settling in, too.